MISTY HOLLOW MASSACRE

CAROL ERICSON

D0815319

MISTY HOLLOW MASSACRE

CAROL ERICSON

Chapter One

The small boy in front of her chewed on his lower lip and kicked his foot against the leg of the chair, tapping out a staccato beat. He blinked his eyes as his floppy brown hair tangled with his eyelashes.

Hannah's fingers tingled with an urge to brush the sticky strands from his face, but his stiff posture screamed hands off.

Instead of initiating physical contact, Hannah smiled and held up a juice box with a straw poking out of the top. "Are you sure you don't want something to drink, Sheldon?"

Sheldon's tongue lodged in the corner of his mouth, as his eyes darted from Hannah's face to the juice box. His restless leg stopped its assault on the chair leg for a second before resuming. He wanted the juice.

Hannah held it out toward him, within his reach. "Go ahead. Take it."

He snatched the juice box from her hand, as if he feared she'd take it back. Then he shoved the miniature straw in his mouth and sucked so hard, the box collapsed.

Maybe the boy hadn't responded to her earlier questions because he'd been dehydrated. Hannah pointed to the oversize bag at her feet. "Would you like another? I have lots more."

He shook his head, and Hannah eked out a small sigh. Progress.

"When was the last time you saw your mommy, Sheldon?"

His eyes widened, and his face blanched, making his coffee colored freckles stand out on his nose and cheeks.

Hannah's stomach lurched. Had Sheldon witnessed something unspeakable? "Did you have dinner with your mom… the last night you saw her?"

"Pizza."

That meshed with the pizza box in the living room of Zoey's mobile home. Sheldon remembered what he ate for dinner that night and probably had eaten with his mom, as the box was empty. As were the five beer bottles, so Zoey could've had company—or not. Polishing off five beers in an evening would be teetotalism for Zoey Grady.

Hannah swallowed her judgment. "I love pizza. What's your favorite kind of pizza?"

Sheldon stuck the straw from the juice box back in his mouth and nibbled on the end of it with his front teeth, wrinkling his nose like a little rabbit.

Hannah went back to the direct questions. "Did your mom tuck you in for bedtime after dinner? Read you a story?"

Sheldon spit the straw out of his mouth. "Mommy's dead."

Tears pricked the back of Hannah's eyes. "I know, sweetie."

Sheldon curled his legs beneath him, slumped to the side of the chair and closed his eyes. She probably wouldn't be able to get any more out of him today.

The soft knock on the door didn't rouse Sheldon from his

position but gave Hannah a start. Typically, nobody ever interrupted a session, but there was nothing typical about this session and she and Sheldon were in a room at the hospital, not her office where she had toys and games to entice even the most reticent little patient.

She said in a hushed tone, "I'm going to answer the door, Sheldon."

The boy didn't move one muscle, so Hannah pushed up from her chair and crossed the room. She cracked open the door, blocking Deputy Fletcher's view of Sheldon. "Any news?"

"The social worker is here and wants to take custody of the boy, Dr. Maddox. His doc cleared him to be discharged. Nothing physically wrong with him, except he's a little underweight." Fletcher shrugged his own narrow shoulders.

Hannah had noticed Sheldon's spindly legs and knobby knees, but many young children burned calories faster than their bodies had time to store them. She'd consult with Dr. Robbins to find out the extent of Sheldon's malnourishment.

Fletcher shifted his stance to see around her body. "Did you get anything out of him?"

She put a finger to her lips and shuffled toward Fletcher, pushing him back a few steps into the antiseptic hallway. Sheldon might be nonresponsive, but it didn't mean he couldn't hear everything they said. "Not much. He did eat pizza with his mom that night, so she was alive for dinner. He knows she's dead. Did the officer on the scene tell him? Do you know if he left the house at all?"

Holding out his hands, Fletcher said, "Whoa, whoa. You need to talk to Detective Howard Chu from Seattle PD Homicide."

Hannah glanced over her shoulder at Sheldon, still curled

into a ball, and then stepped toward Fletcher, pulling the door closed behind her. "Detective Chu wasn't first on the scene, was he? The time it probably took him to get out to the island puts him farther behind than I am. If I'm going to help Sheldon, I need to know what happened out there."

"Dr. Maddox?" The other officer who'd been at the crime scene approached her and Fletcher. "I'm Deputy Tony Hill."

"Deputy Hill." Hannah nodded. "Can you give me a little more background here? I didn't get much before Sheldon was handed off to me."

"I know. Sorry about that. Sheriff Hopkins asked me to call you as soon as Doc Robbins was done examining him today. Social services wasn't ready for him yet, so I kind of dumped him on you."

"He's a child. You didn't dump him on me, Hill." Hannah pressed her lips into a thin line. Good thing she'd closed that door.

"Right, sorry." The red-faced deputy jerked his thumb over his shoulder. "Before the social worker takes him, the sheriff wanted me to brief you both at the same time."

"Perfect." She spun around to Fletcher, who was on his phone. "Can you sit with Sheldon?"

"Me?" Fletcher's voice squeaked as he clapped his phone to his chest. "Is he sleeping? What am I supposed to do?"

Hannah leveled a finger at the phone clutched in his claw-like hand. "Why don't you show him that game you were playing?"

Fletcher peeled the phone from his body and eyed it. "Really? You think he'd like that?"

"He's a boy. If it's a game where you blast things to smithereens, he'll love it." She patted his arm.

"Got it." Fletcher took a deep breath and entered the room.

Hannah peered over the deputy's shoulder at Sheldon, still curled up, but eyes wide open. She gave him a little wave before Fletcher closed the door.

"You think Fletcher will be okay in there with the boy?" She raised her eyebrows at Hill.

"Fletch?" He snorted. "He's a kid himself."

"Who's the social worker?" she asked. She knew most of them and definitely had her preferences.

"It's Ms. Jacobson. She's in a room downstairs." Hill gave her a sideways glance as she matched him stride for stride down the hallway. "Are you...um... Sheriff Maddox's daughter?"

"I am." She took in his smooth cheeks and bright eyes. "He was before your time."

"He was, but he's kind of a legend on Dead Falls Island—Mad Dog Maddox."

"You have no idea." Hannah clenched her jaw and folded her arms, hoping to bring an end to the subject of her father.

"Sheriff Hopkins says..." Hill trailed off and rolled his lips inward as if trying to trap the words in his mouth. He ended up mumbling, "Never mind."

Deputy Hill didn't have to continue. She had a pretty good idea what Hopkins had to say about her father, Hopkins's predecessor. It's nothing she didn't already know, and half agree with.

Hill kept his mouth shut on the elevator ride down one floor, and as he led her to the office where Maggie Jacobson waited.

As they entered the room, Maggie glanced up from her phone, her face white. "Hey, Hannah. This is Zoey Grady's son? She's really dead?"

"I'm afraid so, Maggie." Hannah crossed the room to

shake the other woman's hand as Maggie half rose from her chair. "Murdered. We don't know yet if Sheldon saw anything, but he knows his mom is gone."

Maggie cupped her face with one hand. "That's terrible. And you? How are you holding up?"

Hill jerked his head toward Hannah, but she avoided his gaze.

"Awful situation, of course, but…you know. It's been a while."

"That's true." Maggie ran her hands over her gauzy skirt. "What can you tell us, Deputy Hill?"

"A dog walker discovered Zoey Grady's body this morning, at about seven, outside her trailer at the mobile home park. Called 911. Looked like she'd been murdered elsewhere, probably inside her home, and dragged to that location. She was wearing pajamas, no ID, but I recognized her and knew she lived in one of the trailers on that property. Knew she had a kid, too. We went to her place and found the boy in bed."

Maggie exchanged a look with Hannah. "Awake or asleep?"

"Eyes wide open." Hill lifted one shoulder. "Didn't say one word to me or Deputy Fletcher. I haven't heard the kid speak yet."

Hannah swallowed. "That could be a side effect of the trauma from his mother dying or the neglect he likely faced."

"That's possible?" Hill's forehead creased.

Hannah closed her lips on a sigh. Her dad's deputies would've been more knowledgeable than this—but these weren't Sheriff Maddox's deputies. Sheriff Maddox was dead.

Maggie barked, "It's not uncommon."

Hannah folded her hands in her lap, not wanting to pass any judgment on a dead woman.

Maggie had no such sensibilities. "Zoey Grady—mother of the year."

She immediately clapped a hand over her mouth. "Sorry, Hannah."

"I told you." Hannah waved a hand in the air. "Long time ago."

Hill's gaze darted between the two of them before continuing, "Anyway, once I called it in and Hopalong—I mean, Sheriff Hopkins—called me back, he told me to contact you, Dr. Maddox, once the kid was done here at the hospital."

Hannah covered her smirk with her hand at the use of Sheriff Hopkins's nickname. The man didn't have a limp like the fictional cowboy, but when he got excited, he got a kick to his gait, which led to the nickname. He hated it.

"Cause of death?" Maggie looked hopeful, but Hill disappointed her.

"We're not going public with that, ma'am." He hunched forward. "But I did see blood at the scene."

Hill couldn't tell them much more, but Maggie took copious notes, anyway. When Hill finished, Maggie snapped her notebook shut. "We'll secure Sheldon, Hannah. Settle him with one of our foster families, but we—and the cops, I assume—will want you to continue sessions with him."

"Of course." Hannah pushed up from her chair. "I'll come along to introduce you to Sheldon and provide some continuity to the transition, so he doesn't feel as if he's being shuttled from one person to another."

The transfer of Sheldon from one authority figure to another went well, in large part due to the efforts of Deputy

Fletcher. The game on his phone had put Sheldon in much better spirits.

After Maggie took over and as the deputies gave Hannah a ride back to the station, Hannah made sure to compliment Fletcher on his connection with Sheldon, and even found out that the deputy's first name was Niles.

She tapped on the window of the patrol vehicle, as it rolled into the parking lot of the station. "I left my car in the lot to the right."

As the deputies swung around to pull next to her car, a tall man strode toward the station, brushing his longish, black hair from his face.

Hannah's mouth dropped open as she drank in the sight of the man who still plagued her dreams. "What's Jed Swain doing here?"

Hill threw the car into Park. "What do you think? Zoey Grady was murdered. You know the history. Swain is our prime suspect."

Chapter Two

Jed's head jerked to the side at the sound of the car door slamming, and he narrowed his eyes at the two deputies ambling toward him. He didn't need an escort. He'd come to the station voluntarily when Hopkins had called him earlier. As soon as he heard the news, he figured he'd be on the short list and wanted to clear things up before the situation spun out of control. He knew only too well how that worked.

A female passenger got out of the back seat, and Jed almost tripped and fell on his face when he saw Hannah Maddox raise a tentative hand in his direction, her light brown hair whipping across her face. He didn't need to see her face. He'd recognize her anywhere.

What the hell had she been doing in the squad car? Did this town have to consult a Maddox every time someone committed a crime on Dead Falls Island?

He didn't want to stop. Didn't want to see her. But his body operated separately from his brain—just as it always had when it came to Hannah.

He nodded at the two deputies as they walked past him, and then shoved his hands in the pockets of his jeans to await the moment he'd both dreaded and desired for the past three years.

As she approached him, she tucked her hair behind her ears and offered a tremulous smile. "I—I didn't know you were back on the island. How are you? You look...great."

A flush rose to her cheeks as she finished, clutching her purse strap with both hands, her shoulders stiff.

"Got back a few weeks ago, and they're already accusing me of murder." The corner of his mouth curled. Did she expect him to make this easy on her after what her father did to him?

"Oh, surely not." She brought her fingertips to her lush mouth, her lips a pink rose color that owed everything to nature and not a tube of lipstick. He'd once fed her cherries just to see the purple juice stain those lips before kissing them.

He cleared his throat. "Just dropping by to get ahead of this. I had an alibi for last night."

"I didn't ask." She dropped her lashes. "Are you at the cabin?"

"It needs work. I'm at Tate and Astrid's until I fix the roof." He squared his shoulders.

"I wasn't checking your alibi," she said in a firmer voice, a militant light in her hazel eyes as her gaze met his.

He jerked his thumb over his shoulder. "I gotta go inside and talk to Hopkins, so he can tell that detective from Seattle to take me off his short list."

"Can we have dinner sometime? Catch up?"

"Thanks to your father, I went to prison for five years and got out three years ago. We're caught up." He turned away before those shimmering eyes could soften the ball of fury in his heart.

Jed pushed through the front door of the Dead Falls Sheriff's Department. Too small to properly investigate a homicide, they'd called in the Seattle PD Homicide Division to help out. Maybe if Sheriff Maddox had done that eight years ago, he never would've gone to prison.

He hunched over the counter. "Jed Swain to see Sheriff Hopkins."

The deputy manning the front desk held up one finger as he hit a key on his computer with the other. "Give me a minute."

When the printer in the corner came to life, the deputy grabbed the phone on his desk. "Jed Swain to see you, sir."

When he hung up, he wheeled his chair toward the printer, propelling it with his feet. "He'll be right out. He's expecting you."

Jed took a step back and shuffled toward the swinging half door that led to the offices in the back. He had a familiarity with this station he'd never wanted and nothing had changed—except him and the man in the sheriff's office.

Hopkins emerged from the back, hoisting his khaki pants over a prominent belly. He'd come from a midsize town in California, and the residents of Dead Falls Island didn't hold him in high esteem. But Jed would take anyone over Sheriff Maddox.

"Mr. Swain, thanks for coming." Hopkins bumped open the swinging door, extending his hand for a shake.

Jed moved in and grasped his hand. "Sheriff."

"Let's talk in my office." Hopkins held the door open for Jed, and he squeezed past the sheriff's girth, then hung back, waiting for Hopkins to lead the way.

He followed Hopkins back to the same office at the end of the short hallway that Maddox had occupied. Jed's gaze swept the office as Hopkins sat behind the same desk in the same chair with the same view out the window. He studied the photos on the shelf behind Hopkins—a wedding photo with Hopkins as the proud father of the bride, a gray-haired woman clutching a baby to her ample breast, and Hopkins and that same woman smiling on a tropical beach. He exhaled a long breath. No pretty brunette in braces or with a cap and gown. At least the pictures were different from the last time he sat here.

Hopkins spread his hands in front of him. "You understand why we have to go through this exercise, right? You and Zoey Grady have a history—and it ain't a pretty one. It's not because uh…you're…um…"

"An ex-con?" Jed's hands curled into fists at his side, well away from Hopkins's gaze. "Yeah, I get it."

"So, you're staying with Tate and Astrid Mitchell and were there last night?" Hopkins scribbled something on a pad of paper.

"That's right. I'm fixing up my cabin, and it's not inhabitable yet. Tate's with the forestry department where I'm thinking of applying for a job, and he invited me to stay with him and his sister until my place is ready."

"And what did you all do that night?" Hopkins steepled his fingers and peered at Jed over the apex.

"Had a barbecue. Tate and I stayed up kind of late, and then I hit the sack around one o'clock."

"Had some beers? Boozed it up and passed out?" Hopkins raised his untamed eyebrows.

Jed flexed his fingers. "I don't drink. Tate and I stayed up late going over some scenarios for the job. He might've had a few beers, but nobody passed out."

"All right. All right." Hopkins adjusted his glasses and tossed his pen onto his blotter. "We have Tate Mitchell's number. We'll just corroborate, and I'll pass the info on to

Detective Chu. If he wants to ask you anything else, I'm sure he will."

"Don't know why he would." Jed shrugged. "I haven't seen Zoey in years, not even once since I've been back these few weeks."

"I'll add that to my notes for Chu." Hopkins smacked his desk. "That's all I have, Mr. Swain."

Hopkins walked him to the lobby where Jed caught the furtive glances of a few deputies. He set his jaw and straightened his spine. He survived a false imprisonment. Suspicious glances from a couple of small-town deputies didn't faze him.

But seeing Hannah Maddox in the parking lot had rocked his world.

Before heading back to the Mitchells', he drove to his cabin to check up on the roofers. The foreman pointed out a few areas where termites had destroyed the wood and Jed approved the purchase of more materials.

He stepped into the kitchen and took a few more measurements for the cabinets and read some notes the electrician left him. With the work on his own roof and other repairs almost done, he'd be leaving the Mitchells' place in a few weeks.

They'd provided him with an ironclad alibi, though, and he could breathe a sigh of relief to know that Sheriff Hopkins would be looking elsewhere for Zoey Grady's killer.

Later that afternoon, when he got to Tate's house, he sat for a minute, gripping the steering wheel. He couldn't summon much sympathy for Zoey, even though he knew she'd been one messed up person—even before her false accusations against him. But after? He'd heard she'd spiraled out of control—drugs, booze, public fights.

Guilt had a way of eating at you and eventually destroying you. He'd also heard Sheriff Maddox had died of cancer after his retirement. Had it been guilt, in his case, that had eaten away at him?

Something hit his window, and he jumped. Astrid's son, Olly, had his nose smashed against the glass, and Jed flattened his hand against the window before cracking open the door.

"Better move, Olly, or I'm gonna hit you with the door."

The boy danced backward, holding a fish on a line in one hand. "Mom let me go fishing and look what I caught."

Jed eyed the small, silvery fish glinting in the sun. "Looks like you got dinner."

"Olly, stop waving that thing around." Astrid stepped onto the porch, and she folded her arms over her stomach. "Sorry, Jed."

"No worries." Jed slammed the door of the truck, and it was Astrid's turn to jump. Tate's sister was as skittish as he was.

"How'd it go with Hopkins?" She rubbed her arms as if she had a chill, despite the sun beating down on them.

"It went okay. Expect a call—you and Tate."

"We got it covered." She darted a gaze at her son, studying his prize catch. "That poor woman. Do they have any leads? She has a son, right?"

"If they have any leads, they're not gonna tell me." He ruffled Olly's unkempt blond hair as he passed him on the porch. "She did have a son, younger than yours."

"That's awful. I know Zoey had some on-again, off-again relationship with Chase Thompson, and he is bad news." Astrid glanced over Jed's head toward the road. "I hope they catch whoever did this, but I don't think people have much faith in Sheriff Hopkins."

"He called in Seattle PD. Some detective is going to be working the case. He's probably the one who's gonna call you and Tate."

"We got you covered, brother." Tate appeared at the door of the cabin, the sun lighting up his blond hair as much as it did the scales on the fish. "I heard some interesting news."

Astrid dug her fingers into her son's shoulder. "C'mon, Olly, let's clean that out back, and I'll add it to our dinner."

Jed watched Astrid and Olly turn the corner of the cabin with narrowed eyes, and then turned back to Tate. "What news do you have that Astrid didn't want to be around to hear?"

"She already knows." Tate's mouth quirked into that stupid frat boy smile. "Hannah Maddox is involved with the case."

Jed's pulse ticked up, but he kept his face bland. "Really? I thought she was some kind of shrink. Is she a part-time cop now, too?"

Tate whistled. "The animosity. It wasn't Hannah's fault Zoey falsely accused you and Hannah's father happened to be the sheriff who investigated the case and arrested you. Besides, I can see right past the hard stare and firm jaw. You still want her."

Jed opened his mouth and then snapped it shut. He rubbed his jaw, a trick the prison psychologist had taught him to rein in his anger and give him seconds to cool down. "How is Hannah involved?"

"The sheriff's department has her working with the boy, Sheldon. He was home when Zoey was killed, and they haven't figured out if he saw or heard anything."

"That's tough for the kid." Jed shot a sideways look at Tate, who'd experienced his own childhood trauma.

"Yeah, it is." The bright look in Tate's blue eyes faded for a second or two. "Astrid's planning another surprise for you, but I know you don't like surprises. That's why she hightailed it out of here."

The knots in Jed's gut, still not completely loosened from his trip to the sheriff's department, tightened. "What surprise?"

Tate pointed to a rattletrap old truck bouncing down the road to the house. "She invited Hannah for dinner."

"Damn it." Jed ran a hand through his hair. "I already saw Hannah earlier and thought I made my feelings clear."

"Your feelings for Hannah have always been clear, dude." Tate stuck up a hand in a wave. "I don't think you're fooling anyone—not even Hannah."

Jed ground his back teeth. Then he'd just have to try harder.

Hannah stepped out of the truck with a plastic bag dangling from her fingers. "Hello. I brought some potato salad, but it's not homemade as Astrid's invite was last minute."

Jed dug his heels into the wooden step. So, she hadn't known about this invitation when he ran into her at the sheriff's station?

"Homemade?" Tate pushed past Jed, still rooted to the porch. "Hell, before Astrid and Olly moved in a few months ago, I don't think I even ate homemade potatoes."

"A true bachelor." Hannah gave Tate a quick hug, peering at Jed over Tate's shoulder. "We meet again, Jed."

"Yeah, Tate told me you're working with Zoey's kid. Isn't that a conflict of interest, or something?" He folded his arms, not budging from his position on the porch.

"Uh, not really." She shifted the bag from one hand to the other. "It's not like Zoey and I were close…at the end. I'd never even met Sheldon before—just saw him around."

Astrid emerged from the side of the cabin, holding her hands in front of her. "Hi, Hannah. I was helping Olly clean his fish and my hands are disgusting, or I'd give you a hug."

"Thanks for the consideration." Hannah's tongue darted from her mouth and swept across her bottom lip. "Do you need any help with dinner? I brought some potato salad."

"Perfect. Tate's just grilling burgers and bratwurst. Is that okay?"

"Sounds good to me." Hannah finally pushed her designer sunglasses to the top of her head, scooping back her brown curls from her face in the process.

As Astrid made for the front door of the cabin, Hannah followed her. When she reached the porch, Jed took a few steps to the side so she wouldn't brush past him on her way inside.

It didn't help. He still caught the light peach scent from her perfume, or maybe it was her shampoo. Whatever. It filled him with a longing so strong, he almost went to his knees.

He somehow moved his legs down the steps of the porch, calling out to Tate, "Do you need help with the grill?"

"Sure." Tate waited for him and thumped him on the back when he caught up. "Give her a chance, man. During the time you were away, I never heard about any boyfriends or serious relationships. She never believed you did it. Never gave up on you."

"That's strange." Jed swallowed hard. "Usually when someone doesn't give up on you, they try to stay in touch. We do get mail in prison. I didn't hear one word from Hannah."

Tate's brow furrowed as he lit the charcoal already piled up on the barbecue. "That's weird. She told me she wrote you all the time, but you never responded."

"Nope. Didn't happen." Jed stared into the flames as they leaped up from the briquettes. "Why did Astrid invite her today? Astrid was ahead of us in school. I didn't know she and Hannah were close."

Jed held up a hand. "Confession time. I invited her."

"Damn, Tate. Are you a forestry agent or a matchmaker?" Jed poked at the flaming coals. "Shouldn't you worry about your own love life, which is basically nonexistent?"

"Me?" Tate thumped his chest with his palm. "I got no problem in that department, brother."

Jed snorted. "I'm not talking about one-night stands."

"Shh." Tate jabbed him in the ribs with a sharp elbow as Astrid and Hannah came around the corner with trays laden with buns, condiments, and sliced tomatoes and onions.

Olly trotted behind them with his cleaned fish on a small plate.

Astrid nodded to her son. "You guys are going to have to grill that fish, too."

"We can manage that." Tate bumped fists with his nephew. "Hand it over, buddy."

By the time they'd grilled all the burgers and brats, and even Olly's fish, Astrid and Hannah had lit another fire in the pit and had arranged some chairs around the blaze.

Although the sun hadn't set yet, the fog from Discovery Bay was rolling inland, blanketing everything with a cool mist.

They all loaded up plates and balanced them on their knees as they crowded around the firepit. Of course, Hannah couldn't talk about her work or patients, even refusing to directly admit she was seeing Sheldon.

In between admonishing Olly and making sure everyone had a full plate, Astrid talked about passing the test for her Realtor's license and Jed talked about his plans for joining Tate with the forestry service.

Astrid shoved a napkin at Olly. "You passed the background investigation and everything, Jed? No problems with your record?"

Jed scratched his chin. "Since I was fully exonerated, I have no record."

Tate said, "But you do have a ton of cash."

Jed kicked Tate's foot and stuffed the rest of his burger into his mouth.

"Oh?" Hannah patted some mustard from the corner of her mouth. "Did you sue the county of San Juan?"

"I did." Jed dropped his chin to his chest in a curt nod. "Got a settlement."

"That's good. I'm glad. I know it can't give you those years back…"

"Or my good name." Jed finished off his soda and crushed the can. "You know there are people on this island who still believe I did it and probably believe I offed Zoey, too."

Astrid jumped up. "C'mon, Olly. Time to get ready for bed. You can read a little extra tonight."

Olly slid from his chair and rubbed his belly. "That fish hit the spot."

Tate threw his head back and laughed. "It did. I'm gonna put you in charge of catching our dinner every night, and right now you're going to help me bring this stuff back in the house and clean up."

Hannah held up her plate. "Give me a few more bites, and I'll help."

Astrid said, "You two sit right where you are. You're our guests and you already did enough to help. Relax and enjoy the fire."

In two minutes flat, the three Mitchells had cleared out, leaving him with Hannah chewing the last few bites of her burger.

The fire crackled, and Hannah's eyes glowed with the flame, the orange licks bringing out the golden highlights in her brown hair.

"What?" She covered the lower half of her face with a napkin. "Do I have grease all over my chin?"

Busted. With an almost physical effort, he dragged his gaze from her face. "Do you work here on the island?"

She crumpled her napkin in one hand and dropped it onto her empty plate. "I have an office here and in Seattle— mostly forensic psychology. I testify in court sometimes. I assist police departments with criminal assessments."

"And you question little boys whose mothers have been murdered." He stretched his hands to the fire, although an internal heat already raged through his body.

"Can't talk about that, but we can talk about you." She put her plate on an empty chair and folded her hands in her lap. "I was thrilled when you were exonerated and released. I—I thought you'd come back to Dead Falls sooner."

"Didn't have anything to come back to." He shrugged. "My mom left the cabin in disrepair, and I moved to California to finish my degree at Cal Poly San Luis Obispo, and then moved to LA for some work. I'd been in touch with Tate and when he mentioned his department was hiring,

I decided to come back. Could be the worst move of my life—out of many bad moves."

Hannah dropped her gaze and studied her fingernails. "I know you were mad because it was my father who was sheriff during the investigation, but he had a job to do, Jed. He had to follow the evidence."

A muscle twitched at the corner of his eye. Was that why she thought he was mad? Her father just doing his job?

"I guess that's why you never answered my letters from prison." She clasped her hands between her knees and met his eyes without a trace of deception in her own. Had she learned to lie from her old man?

He rubbed the smoke from his eyes. "I never got any letters from you, Hannah."

She drew in a quick breath and coughed on the same smoke floating from the dying embers. "What are you talking about? I sent you letters weekly—at first. When you didn't answer, I cut back to monthly, then holidays and then I gave up."

Cocking his head, he repeated, "I never got any letters."

"Would they... Would the prison confiscate them for some reason?" Released from their own prison, her hands flailed in the air. "I sent you letters, Jed. I did."

"Did you mail them yourself?" He sat back in his chair, folding his arms over his chest, a tightness forming there.

"You know there aren't many mailboxes outside town. I gave them to my mom when she went into town."

"You mean when she used to go into town to visit your father and bring him lunch. Did she use the mailbox outside the sheriff's station?" He grunted. "That makes sense."

"What are you saying?" She jumped up from her chair and knocked it over. "My mother would never have done anything with those letters other than what I asked her to do."

"Really, Hannah?" He stood up, facing her across the fire, feeling a strange kind of headiness knowing she *had* written to him when he was incarcerated. "Your mother was completely under your father's thumb, and you know that."

"So now you're saying my father convinced her not to send those letters?"

"It's so obvious." He squeezed the back of his neck. So obvious, he didn't know why he hadn't thought of it before.

"Why is it so obvious, Jed? You think my father wouldn't have wanted me to correspond with a convict? Even you?" Her voice wavered at the end.

"Of course, he wouldn't, Hannah. He hated that we had started dating so much, he set me up for the rape of Zoey Grady."

Chapter Three

The blood drained from Hannah's head, and she threw out an arm to steady herself. Jed took a half step forward, and then drew back. Of course, he did.

She licked her lips and tried to swallow against her dry throat. Jed was wrong. Is this what he'd believed all these years? Is this why he'd never reached out to her?

"Th-that's absurd, Jed. My father was a good cop. He never would've—" she waved her arms over her head "—manufactured or falsified evidence against you or anyone else. Maybe he didn't approve of our relationship, but that was probably more because he thought I was too young to get serious with anyone. It wasn't *you*."

Shoving his hands in his pockets, Jed kicked at one of the logs that bordered the firepit. "You're right. Nobody was good enough for his *princess*—especially me. No-good, alcoholic father, floozy for a mother, cops called out to our place all the time."

Hannah dug her heels into the dirt. "You are not your parents. You never were. Dad knew that."

"Did he?" Jed cocked his head, a smile that looked more like a snarl twisting his lips. "He was smart. I'll give the old sheriff that. Figured if he objected too much, you'd grit your teeth and see me just to spite him. He went for the foolproof plan, saw his opportunity with Zoey's allegations and took it."

"I refuse to believe my father set you up for a crime you didn't commit." She stamped her foot. "He just wouldn't do something like that."

"What about your letters to me? If you really wrote them, I never received them."

"*If* I really wrote them?" She wedged a fist on her hip, her blood simmering. "I'm telling you I sent you letters. Are you calling me a liar, too?"

"Think about it, Hannah." Jed tapped the side of his head. "You wrote me letters and gave them to your mom to mail. She takes them into town, where she visits your dad every day, and what? Drops them in the mailbox where they magically get lost on their way to the Washington State Penitentiary? Or does she leave them in the mail outbox at the station where your father, the sheriff, conveniently snatches them from the pile and destroys them?"

Hannah swallowed the scream building in her chest. She wanted to refute Jed's claim. She wanted to defend her father. But she couldn't—not entirely. Not after what she'd discovered about her father after his death—what she'd always known about him when he was alive.

"How's it going out here?" Astrid approached the firepit, tucking a strand of hair behind her ear. She stumbled to a stop, glancing between Hannah's and Jed's faces. "You let the fire die down."

"In a way." Hannah brushed off her jeans. "I'm ready to head out. Do you need help with anything, Astrid?"

"We have everything under control. Doesn't look like it, but Tate is pretty good around the house. Must be all those years as a bachelor." Astrid gave them an awkward smile and waved a hand over her shoulder. "I'll get Tate out here."

Hannah didn't want to be left alone outside with Jed. She had too many thoughts to sort out and didn't need him confusing her. She made a move to follow Astrid back into the house, but Tate saved them the trouble.

After a quick glance at Jed's stony face, Tate said, "Are you leaving so soon, Hannah?"

If Tate thought he was going to play matchmaker for her and Jed, he didn't know the depths of Jed's hatred for her family. Had Jed told anyone else about his suspicions?

Hannah cleared her throat. "It's really kind of late, Tate, and I have some work to do at home."

"Okay, then. Bring it in." Tate opened his arms, and Hannah walked into them, pressing her tingling nose against his chest. Why couldn't Jed be more like Tate? Tate wanted to please everyone, and Jed couldn't care less. Had prison made him hard? He'd always been a rebel, but he'd had a sweetness about him that attracted all the girls—including her best friend at the time, Zoey Grady.

She sniffled. "You need to put out that fire once and for all. It's just a smoke pit now."

"I'll take care of it, Tate." Jed stirred the dying embers with a metal rod, sending a shower of sparks skyward.

Tate gave her another squeeze. "Good to see you, Hannah."

When he released her, Hannah gave Astrid a quick side hug. "Thanks for having me."

"Are you driving home alone?" Jed jabbed a finger toward the old truck she used to spare her car some of the rougher terrain through the forest and for times like this when her car was in the shop for service.

"I drove here alone. How else am I supposed to get back?" She turned her back on him and trudged toward the truck, her sneakers crunching dried twigs and leaves into the ground.

"Now that we all know I didn't do it, there's a killer loose in Dead Falls, and the cops don't have a clue. It's not safe out there at night—alone."

Hannah tripped over an exposed root and flattened her hand on the hood of the truck to save herself from an embarrassing fall. "I'll be fine. I'm sure Zoey's murder had something to do with the drug trade here on the island."

When she opened her door, she turned to wave at Astrid and Tate. Jed kept her pinned in his gaze as she hopped into the truck. His pumped-up physique and tattoo snaking down his arm gave him a menacing appearance. Yeah, prison had changed him—but it wasn't her father's fault.

She turned the key, and the truck growled at her but the engine didn't turn over. She took her foot off the gas, gave it a few seconds and tried again. The growl turned into a scream.

A thump on her hood made her jump. She peered at Jed and Tate through her windshield. She popped the release, and the hood squealed as they opened it.

They tinkered for several minutes and had her start up again, to no avail. She clambered from the truck and poked her head around the open hood.

"What's the verdict?"

Jed slammed the hood and the truck shuddered. "Verdict is, you're not driving this truck tonight. Even if we could get it started, you're not driving this heap home with a murderer on the loose."

Hannah cast a hopeful look at Tate, but he was already

thumping Jed on the back. "Can you give her a ride home, buddy? I have some reports to do."

"Yeah." Jed fished his keys from his front pocket and swung them around his finger. "Hop in. I don't think it's a bad idea, anyway, for someone to see you home safely."

At least he didn't totally hate her. He didn't want to see her dead. "I can always try to call up a car."

Astrid snorted. "Here? That'll take some time."

Jed had already moved to his black truck and swung open the passenger door. "C'mon, Hannah."

Did she have a choice? Did she want a choice?

She lifted her hand at Astrid and Tate. "Thanks again. My turn next time."

Brushing past Jed to climb into the truck, she caught a whiff of stark masculinity—a woodsy smell combined with the smoky undertones of the fire.

He got behind the wheel, and the engine turned over smoothly in the brand-new truck. Had he bought it with his settlement money?

As he turned onto the road that led away from the Mitchells' place, Hannah smoothed her hands along the leather seat. "Nice ride."

She was determined to steer this conversation toward generic small talk. She didn't want to argue with Jed, didn't want to get into a defense of her father.

"Yeah, I bought it a year ago, along with a condo in San Luis Obispo." He brushed his black hair from his face. "My attorney got a nice cut from my lawsuit against the state. My cut was even bigger."

Hannah swallowed. So much for generic small talk. "I know it can't compensate for what you went through, but I'm glad you got something out of it."

She pressed her lips together. That sounded so stupid. That's not what she meant to say. Massaging her right temple, she said, "I…"

"Never mind. I know what you meant." He slid a glance at her. "Headache?"

Trying to talk to him was giving her a headache. She'd felt awkward talking to him before, but now that she knew he suspected her father of setting him up, she had no idea how to navigate a conversation with him.

She rubbed her eyes. "Probably that smoke. When did Astrid move back? I'd heard her marriage didn't work out."

"You could say that." He flexed his fingers on the steering wheel, the bird tattoo he had between his thumb and forefinger flapping its wings. "She moved in with Tate a few months ago. The living situation works for Tate when he gets sent to other locations to battle fires."

"And you'll be joining him soon?"

"I'm in the process. Just one more exam to take before I start the academy." He hunched his shoulders. "I've been doing a little PI work in the meantime. Got my license and have been doing a few jobs."

"That must be interesting." She let out a breath, happy to be talking about something other than Zoey, prison or her father.

"Some divorce cases, insurance fraud—that kind of thing." He drummed his thumbs against the steering wheel. "Nothing too exciting."

"I would think you'd be done with excitement." She bit her bottom lip. Why couldn't she just leave it alone?

Jed's jaw tightened and took the last turn to her house so tightly, the tires squealed in protest. "Here we are. Why'd you drive the old truck? Is that all you have on the island?"

She scanned her empty driveway. "My other car is in the shop. I figured I'd have the truck as backup. I can probably get Jimmy at the shop to tow the truck in for me and trade me one car for the other."

"Bad luck." He pulled into the driveway, and she suspected he scrambled from the car so fast so that he wouldn't have to listen to her tell him he didn't need to see her to the front door.

He'd always seen her to the front door—not quite the uncouth barbarian her father would have her believe. If she were being honest with herself, she had to admit that when the relationship between her and Jed had turned romantic, her father seemed to find all kinds of excuses for sending her off the island.

She shoved open the passenger door before he had time to come around and open it for her. Two could play this game.

She joined him as he gazed up at the peaked roof and long windows of the house. She'd always been slightly embarrassed by her family home. Its size and elegance had seemed at odds with the island, but her mother's family had money and her father had embraced that money with gusto. Her mom had been only too happy to hand over the house to Hannah when her dad died and escape to warmer climes.

"Looks the same." Jed shook his head. "Of course, your father wouldn't let me inside at the end, so I could only imagine how the interior had changed from when we were children."

"It's not that…" She stopped when Jed turned his dark gaze on her and waved her hand at the house. "Do you want to have a look now? Mom did a little work, and I did a little more."

Those deep brown eyes glittered before he dropped his lashes. "Maybe another time. Good night, Hannah."

She watched him get into his gleaming truck and then, realizing he wouldn't leave until she went into the house, she spun around and shoved the key into the lock. Only when she had made it inside and had the door closed behind her, did she hear Jed's engine start.

Pressing her back against the door, she let out a long sigh. Jed's presence on Dead Falls was about to complicate her life.

Her cat, Siggy, wound his body around her ankles, and she bent over to scratch under his chin. "I fed you before I left. That's it for you, Sigmund."

She checked all the doors in the big house, her gaze flitting toward the square in the ceiling that led to the attic. She hadn't been up there since her mom moved out, but she'd noticed boxes of her father's old papers up there. Would he have something about Jed's case?

Giving in to temptation, she dragged a step stool from the garage to beneath the attic door and stepped on the bottom rung to reach the hanging string. She gave it a yank. The door sprang open, revealing the folding ladder, already starting its descent.

She grabbed the ladder with one hand and shoved the step stool to the side with her foot. Once she'd fully extended and secured the ladder, she began to climb it, Siggy right behind her.

When she pulled herself into the crawl space, she shook a finger at Siggy. "You'd better hope I don't trap you up here when I leave."

She couldn't quite straighten to her full height and settled for walking a bit hunched over, like a Cro-Magnon, as she scanned the space with her cell phone light. She should've brought a proper flashlight with her.

To read the writing on the sides of the boxes, her father's dark scrawl, Hannah dropped to her knees and squinted at the letters.

Siggy purred beside her with excitement, and Hannah stroked his gray stripes. "I'm counting on you to keep the mice and spiders at bay up here."

Her heart thumped when she spotted a few boxes indicating case numbers and names, all dated. It's not like her father would've been able to take the case files home with him when he retired, but she knew he kept his own notes about cases—notes that never made it into the official files.

She squinted at a few old, frayed boxes with the name *Keldorf* written on them and some ancient date. Her father really had done this for quite some time.

Glancing to the right of the old boxes, she felt her heart jump when that August date from eight years ago that changed her life and Jed's jumped out at her. She crouched on her haunches to shove the boxes on top of the August box out of the way. The flurry of dust she dislodged made her nose twitch.

As she reached for the box, her cell phone rang beside her. When she looked at the phone and saw Maggie Jacobson's name, she sucked in a sharp breath, choking on the dust. Had Sheldon opened up to Maggie already?

She wiped a grimy hand against the thigh of her jeans and answered the phone. "What's up, Maggie?"

Ignoring the pleasantries, the social worker jumped right in. "God, I hate to admit this, but Sheldon Grady is gone."

"Gone?" Hannah's sharp tone caused Siggy to flatten his ears and flick his tail in disgust. "What do you mean?"

"I mean, he snuck out of my house. I've searched everywhere and can't find him."

Hannah was already walking on her knees toward the open square, pushing the August box in front of her, leaving the others behind. "Have you called the sheriff's department?"

"Done. They have a patrol car scouring the area now."

"Maggie, maybe the killer snatched him." Hannah sneezed.

Maggie made a humming sound. "I thought about that, but I don't think so. Everything was too silent for someone to break into my house and take Sheldon."

"I hope you're right—not that Sheldon escaping on his own is a good thing. I'm going to head out now and join the search. I knew his mother, and I talked to him." Hannah backed out of the attic, tipping the box into her arms. Leaning the front of her body against the ladder, she steadied herself. She waved one arm at Siggy, shooing him from the crawl space, and then descended the rest of the way.

Fur flying, Siggy jumped past her, and Hannah planted her feet on the floor, still talking to Maggie. "Maybe he went back home, Maggie. As awful as it was the last time he was there, it's all he knows."

"You might be right." Maggie's voice faded out and then came back. "You have that address?"

"Not on me. Look in your files. I just know how to get to the mobile home park from my house, so I'm heading there now. How long has he been missing?"

"Half an hour, maybe. Do you think he knows the way?"

"I'm sure he does. Most kids on the island know their way around, and Zoey's place isn't that far from yours."

Hannah left the attic open and pounced on her purse. "I'll meet you over there…and tell the police."

Hannah ended the call and stuffed her phone in her purse. She eyed the box on the floor as Siggy rubbed against it. She didn't need her cat getting into those files before she had a chance to peek at them.

She slung her purse over her shoulder and hoisted the box in her arms. She carried it to the pantry off the kitchen, dropped it inside with a thump and closed the door. As she crossed the room, she tripped to a stop. She didn't have any transportation.

Before she had time to think, she reached for the phone and put in Jed's number, which she'd committed to memory. Would he pick up without knowing the caller?

After two rings, she heard an accusatory, rough voice. "Who is this?"

"It's Hannah." She held her breath.

"How'd you get my number?" Suspicion still edged his voice.

"Long story. Hey, Zoey's son, Sheldon, slipped away from the social worker. I think he might be at his home. Do you think you can give me a ride over there? The social worker's on her way and so are the police, so you don't need to stay there. Just drop me off." She paused into the silence. "Do you think you can do that?"

"I'll be right there. I'm not that far." He cleared his throat. "I made a stop on the way back to Tate's cabin."

"Thanks, Jed. I'll be waiting out front." Had he made a stop at that lookout over the falls where they used to meet? She dismissed the thought as soon as it surfaced. She was the only one who seemed to want to relive old memories.

Hannah barreled out the front door and raced to the edge

of her driveway. Ten minutes later, Jed's truck roared up the street. The lookout was about ten minutes away, so maybe he *had* taken a detour to the falls.

She waved him down, as if he weren't here for her. Before the truck even stopped, she grabbed the handle of the passenger door. She dove inside and slammed the door. "Thanks so much. He's just a boy."

"You don't have to sell it to me, Hannah." He peeled away from the entrance to her driveway. "I would help any child—regardless of his parents."

"I know you would." She brushed the hair from her face and peered at him. "Do you think it's a good guess that he went home?"

"Probably. Where else would he go?" The muscles on his bare forearms tensed. "No matter how wretched your home life is, as a kid, it's all you know."

She blinked. She knew all too well about Jed's home life—drunken father, warring parents, his mother always threatening to go back to the res. When Jed was arrested, his parents disowned him and his mother's people shunned him.

Hannah opened her mouth to give Jed the next direction, but the truck followed the way to Zoey's rundown trailer as if under its own agency. Of course, Jed knew the way to this place that had lodged itself in his history. Like many residents of Dead Falls Island, Zoey had inhabited her family home.

His headlights lit up the yellow tape still ringing the property. The police believed Zoey was attacked in her home and then dragged outside of her house and finished off in the back. They'd labeled that entire area as the crime scene.

Jed's truck jostled through the mobile home park and pulled in front of Zoey's trailer. He cut his engine, leaving on his headlights. Hannah slid from the truck and cupped her hand around her mouth. "Sheldon? Sheldon are you here? It's Dr. Maddox—Hannah. Do you remember me?"

Jed nudged her and pointed to the dilapidated swing set on one side of the trailer, one chain swaying in the breeze-less night.

Hannah crept toward the play area. "Sheldon? I can push you on the swings, if you want."

A slight scuffle came from the brush beyond the swing set but stopped when a patrol car, lights flashing, came careening down the road. Hannah froze and glared over her shoulder. Did the cops believe that was any way to approach a missing, traumatized child?

A smaller car followed, and Maggie emerged, shielding her eyes with one hand. She whispered, "Anything?"

"Maybe in those bushes past the swing set." Hannah turned back toward the noise she'd heard earlier. "Sheldon? We're all here to help you."

The bushes parted, and Sheldon's pale face appeared between the branches.

Hannah eked out a breath. "That's right, sweetheart. Come on out."

Sheldon scrambled from the bushes and tiptoed toward her. Hannah couldn't help herself and closed the gap between them, enfolding Sheldon's thin frame in her arms. "It's okay. Everything's going to be okay."

The boy remained still and listless in her hug and then his little body stiffened, and Hannah feared she'd made a mistake by showing him physical affection. She dropped her arms and scooted away from him.

"Are you all right, Sheldon?"

His eyes grew round, and he lifted a skinny arm, his finger pointing. "That's him."

Hannah whirled around, as Sheldon focused like a laser on Jed, lounging against his truck. Her heart sank. "That's who, sweetheart?"

And then Sheldon howled loud enough for the entire island to hear him. "That's the bad man."

Chapter Four

Jed froze, his fingers digging into his biceps. People had been hurling accusations against him all his life, but this one, from this boy, cut like a straight edge across his throat. The cops had heard Sheldon's voice ring out. The social worker heard it. Hannah had heard it, her wide eyes, glimmering in the dark, pinned on him.

Jed's muscles twitched, the fight-or-flight instinct warring through his body. He clenched his teeth, preparing for one of the cops to make a move and throw him into the back of the patrol car to return to the station for more questioning.

Hannah turned slowly back to the boy and brushed a lock of hair from his eyes. She whispered something to him, and Sheldon shook his head.

The cops had their heads together, murmuring, as they shot him a few glances. He overheard the word *alibi* once, so they must've known he'd been cleared already—but that didn't mean anything on this island. He'd been a fool to return and expect anything to change.

Hannah straightened to her full height and took Sheldon's hand in hers. She led him toward the other woman standing with the cops. She cleared her throat. "Sheldon left a special toy at home, but he couldn't get in the house. I told him we'd get it for him tomorrow. Is that okay, Sheldon?"

He nodded once, his gaze flicking to Jed, still propped up against his truck.

One of the cops jerked his thumb at Jed. "What did Sheldon mean?"

"Maybe you'd better ask him, yourself." Hannah smiled at the boy. "Go ahead and tell them what you told me, and then maybe Miss Maggie will give you a cookie when you get back to her place."

"Nothing wrong with a cookie before bedtime." Maggie rubbed her hands together. "I could use one, myself."

The younger cop kneeled in front of Sheldon. "Why is he a bad man, Sheldon?"

Sheldon rubbed his eye with his fist. "Mommy told me. Said she hated him."

Feeling was mutual, kid. Jed's muscles ached with the tension.

"Did he hurt your mommy, Sheldon? Was he here last night?"

Sheldon shook his head, and Jed released a slow breath. "No. I don't know who hurt my mommy."

"Okay, okay." The cop patted Sheldon on the shoulder awkwardly. "Can you go with…uh… Miss Maggie now?"

Sheldon dropped his chin to his chest and left it there.

Maggie held out her hand. "Cookies?"

Sheldon shuffled his feet toward the social worker and glanced over his shoulder at Hannah before he climbed into the car.

Hannah lifted her hand in a wave.

When Maggie's car pulled into the road, the cops sauntered toward Jed, and he finally pushed off the truck, keeping his arms folded, his hands bunched.

"What do you think that was all about?" The cop's hand hovered near his belt, as if he expected Jed to make a move.

Jed lifted his shoulders. "She falsely accused me of rape. She must've hated me for some reason to do that. Then I was exonerated. That means she was a liar. Didn't make her look so good. And she probably hated me even more. She most likely pointed me out on the street to her son and told him I was a bad man. Mother of the year."

The cop flinched. "She's dead."

Narrowing his eyes, Jed said, "Doesn't make her a good mother."

The inquiring cop's partner coughed. "We're ready to roll. Are you okay, Hannah?"

"I'm good. I'm glad we found Sheldon. Thanks for coming out."

The cops said their goodbyes…to Hannah, and peeled out in their squad car, kicking up gravel in their wake.

His gaze and hers locked for several seconds in the silence. She broke first, tucking her hair behind her ear. "I— I'm sorry you had to go through that. I think that's exactly what happened—Zoey pointed you out to Sheldon, and he remembered what she said. He was already in a heightened state of anxiety when he saw you."

"You don't have to jump to my defense, Hannah." He dug his keys from his front pocket. "I didn't do anything wrong—then or now."

"I know that, but why shouldn't I come to your defense?" She cocked her head. "Especially as you blame my father for your conviction and incarceration."

"Are you considering it a possibility?" He tossed the keys in the air and caught them in his fist.

Hannah moved away from him, scuffing through the twigs and leaves on the ground, and settled on a swing, the chains squeaking with her weight. "It's absurd to think Sheriff Maddox would risk setting you up just to keep us apart. There were other methods he could've employed, ones that weren't illegal, to end our relationship."

Jed followed her to the rusty swing set and gave her a nudge. She lifted her feet and swung forward.

He said, "Who knows? Maybe that wasn't his only motive."

She wedged her feet on the ground again, digging into the dirt with the toe of her shoe. "Zoey's body was found here."

Jed took a step back. "By this swing set?"

Pointing to the rock across from them, she said, "Propped up against that boulder, almost posed."

"Who puts a swing set near a rock like that?" He crouched beside the granite boulder and wrinkled his nose at the brown stain on its surface. Hannah hadn't been kidding. Zoey's blood spilled on this very rock. As he shuffled back on his haunches, a clump of sticky, brown leaves caught his attention.

He leaned over the rock for a closer look, avoiding the bloodstain, using the beam from his phone to illuminate the area. He swallowed when he realized he was staring at a dead bird, ants and maggots already burrowing into its flesh.

"Poor thing."

"What is it?" Hannah had come up behind him and rested her hand on his shoulder as she leaned forward. She dug her fingers into him as she answered her own question. "A bird."

"Looks like Zoey's not the only one who died here." Jed braced his hands on his knees and rose, pocketing his phone.

"That's kind of—" Hannah glanced at the bird again before stepping back "—cold. Your 'mother of the year' comment didn't go over to well with the cops, either. Maybe you should watch what you say about all this."

"Why should I?" His voice came out like a growl, and he closed his eyes and took a deep breath. "The woman tried to destroy my life, and according to her son, she was still bad-mouthing me instead of repenting. I'm not going to pretend she meant anything to me. I'm sorry the kid lost his mother, but I'm not going to lead the mourners."

Hannah whispered, "Should we bury it?"

At the sound of her soft voice, Jed's eyes flew open. "The bird? No. Looks like nature is taking care of returning it to the earth."

Hannah turned her back on the bloodstained rock and the decaying bird and gripped the rusty chain on the swing. "Can you drive me home?"

"Of course." He ran a hand through his messy hair. He'd been so busy stoking his own anger and feelings of injustice, he'd forgotten that Hannah had a little patient to take care of—a boy that was lost, confused and missing his mother. "You didn't have to stay with me. I'm a big boy."

"I just…" She stirred the dirt with the toe of her sneaker. "I just felt so bad when Sheldon pointed the finger at you. When are you ever going to get a break?"

The hitch at the end of her voice cut him, and he spread his arms wide. "Hey, I did get a break. The Law Project saw fit to take up my case and exonerated me. I'm a free man, baby. Can't get a better break than that."

A smile tugged at her lips, as if she didn't know whether to take him seriously. "If you say so."

"I do." He snatched her hand on the way to his truck and almost immediately dropped it. The jolt of electricity that zinged through his body nearly lifted him off his feet.

He glanced at Hannah as she hurriedly folded her arms and stuffed her hands in her armpits. He hadn't been the only one hit by that thunderbolt. He grabbed the handle of the car and yanked the door open before flinging it back. "Whoa. Don't know my own strength."

She hesitated, and he stepped aside so she wouldn't have to squeeze past him. Suddenly, it felt as if they were tiptoeing around each other in a way that hadn't happened at the barbecue. Maybe because he'd been keeping her at arm's length with his surly attitude over dinner. He should go back to surly and save them both a lot of discomfort.

After she settled on the passenger side, he slammed the door harder than he meant to and she jumped in her seat. He couldn't seem to strike the right note with Hannah, and they'd never experienced that in the past.

He took a deep breath before sliding behind the wheel. "How was the boy, anyway?"

Snapping her seat belt, she said, "He told me he'd left a toy behind, but I don't believe that. Maggie got all his favorite toys out. I think he just wanted to check on his mother."

He raised his eyebrows, as he started the engine. "He realizes she's gone, right?"

"He does…on one level." She folded her hands in her lap. "But there's always that other level."

"The one that doesn't want to give up hope. Lucky for me, I always had that belief in prison."

"So did I." She slid a gaze in his direction. "And I wrote you that in those letters you never received."

"I don't know." He gunned the engine, as if that could get him away from Zoey's place faster. "Maybe it's a good thing you didn't have a prison pen pal."

Hannah shook her head, and her hair spilled over her shoulder. "I hate the thought that you believed I didn't write, didn't care…believed you were guilty."

"I never thought that." His hands tensed on the steering wheel. "I figured you knew me well enough to know I'd never hurt a woman like that—not after what my mom went through at the hands of my dad."

"So, you must've thought I didn't care—wanted to be rid of you." She sniffed and pressed the back of her hand against her nose.

He didn't want to wander into this dangerous territory with her. He couldn't have her crying over him and his sob story.

"I thought your old man convinced you to move on." He shrugged. "He always did have a lot of control over you."

She stiffened beside him, and he could almost hear her teeth grinding.

"I moved on because you never answered my letters."

He spread his fingers. "Look, we were sweet on each other. Never even slept together."

Her head whipped around. "Oh, excuse me. I didn't realize that was your criteria for a deep relationship."

He set his face into his prison expression and lifted one shoulder. "It's the truth. Don't beat yourself up that your letters never reached me. I didn't blame you. Never expected to hear from you again."

Hannah huffed through her nose and folded her arms as she turned and stared out the window.

This was the Hannah he wanted, the one he could deal with right now. He couldn't tell her he'd been crushed when she ignored him after his sentencing. He'd wanted her to move on, but it still hurt like hell.

"Okay. You know what?" She tapped on her window. "You can just drop me off at the beginning of the drive here."

"It's almost midnight. Anybody could get onto this property. This gate in the front doesn't do anything about protecting the back and one side that run up against the forest." He aimed the truck up the drive. "As much as the cops want me to be Zoey's killer, I'm not. That means whoever offed her is still out there."

"Knowing Zoey's lifestyle, I'm pretty sure her murder was personal. It might even be that ex-boyfriend of hers. Chase. I'm not worried." She flipped back her hair. "You're just accustomed to your lowlife prison companions."

Hannah strikes back.

He cut the engine and grinned. "Yeah, I did meet quite a few characters during my time behind bars. Not the kind of guys you'd wanna run into, strolling up the long drive to your mansion in the middle of the night."

She stabbed the release on her seat belt and let it slide back into place with a snap. "This is not a mansion."

Hannah's father could've never afforded a property like this on a small-town sheriff's salary, but he'd married into money. Hannah's maternal grandfather had invested big-time in the fledgling Seattle tech industry and his investments had been reaping the rewards ever since. He'd heard that Sheriff Maddox had courted Lizzie Franklin with a single-minded tenacity. Then he played the big man in town, lording it over everyone else as if he'd earned it.

He said, "It's the biggest house on Dead Falls Island. What would you call it? A forest cottage?"

Her nostrils flared, and she almost took the bait but her phone rang in her purse. She plunged her hand into the side pocket of her bag. "What now?"

Jed said, "I hope it's not Sheldon, again."

And he meant it. That kid didn't need any more trauma in his life.

She looked up at him from her phone, her brow crinkled. "It might be. It's one of the deputies from the sheriff's department."

"Take it now in case you need a ride somewhere."

She tapped the phone. "This is Dr. Maddox."

She covered her mouth with one hand and flashed him a wide-eyed glance as the tinny sound of a male voice came over the line.

His stomach flipped.

She nodded. "I understand."

The call must've ended because he didn't hear anything over the line and she'd stopped speaking, but she sat still with the phone pressed to her ear.

"What is it, Hannah? Is it Sheldon?"

She slowly lowered the phone to her lap, cupping it between her hands as if in prayer. "There's been another murder."

Chapter Five

Jed couldn't have done it.

Hannah bit her bottom lip, ashamed at the first thought that flew into her head. A woman had just been murdered—and Jed didn't need her sympathy or protection, anyway. He'd made that heartbreakingly clear.

Jed took a noisy breath beside her. "Who is it this time?"

This time. A shiver ran up Hannah's spine. She swallowed against her dry throat. "Stephanie Boyd, another single mom with a young child. She's a newbie. You wouldn't know her."

"Why did the cops call you? They need your help with her child? Do they think this is linked to Zoey's murder?" He clapped a hand on his forehead. "It would have to be. What are the odds? Two murders in as many days on this island?"

Tapping her phone, she said, "That was an unofficial call. It was an officer from this morning when I saw Sheldon. He was telling me off the record. Didn't give me much, but it has to be tied to Zoey's death, right? I mean, I know Discovery Bay has a brisk little drug trade going on, but we generally don't have serial killers running around the islands."

"You just made a good point." Jed massaged his temple with two fingers. "The murders could have something to do with drugs. We both know Zoey was no stranger to the drug culture. Maybe this… Stephanie was running with the same crowd. Maybe she even knew Chase Thompson. From what I heard, he not only dated Zoey, he dabbled in the drug trade."

"Fletch, the officer, gave me very little. Just a heads up."

"Wait a minute." Jed smacked the steering wheel, causing her to jump for the second time in his car. "Stephanie. What did you say her last name was?"

"Boyd. Stephanie Boyd. Has… Had a daughter."

"Damn." Jed scrambled for his phone that was charging on the console between them. "I think I know this woman."

Hannah's heart picked up the pace in her chest. "How? You met her since you've been back on the island? She's not someone we know from the old days."

"No, but her brother is." He squinted at his phone. "You remember Michael Ramsey?"

"Of course. Few years older than you. Parents got divorced when he was a kid and Mom left the island."

"His mother remarried, had a second family. Stephanie Boyd is Michael's half sister."

"How do you know all this?" She eyed the phone still clutched in his hand, her stomach still queasy that Jed knew the second victim.

"I ran into Michael in LA, of all places. When I told him I was coming back to Dead Falls, he asked me to look in on his half sister, said she was in a bad place." He dropped the phone in his cup holder. "Never got the chance…and now she's in a *really* bad place."

"So, you didn't actually meet Stephanie?" She tucked her own phone in the side pocket of her purse, a tiny breath escaping from between her lips.

He jerked his head to the side. "Worried the cops are gonna come after me for this one, too?"

"Of course not." She brushed an imaginary strand of hair from her cheek. "You were with the Mitchells and me all night, anyway."

"I'm glad you have my alibi all sorted out for me." His lips twisted into a smile.

"Well, this isn't about you, is it?" Why did Jed have to keep jumping on everything she said? Wasn't she allowed to be concerned about him?

He slumped in his seat. "No, it isn't. I'm going to have to call Michael and tell him I never even got around to checking on his sister. Do you think it's a coincidence that Zoey and Stephanie were both single moms?"

"I'm sure of it, indirectly, at least. Their deaths must have something to do with their lifestyles. If Michael was worried about his sister, she was probably mixed up with the wrong people. We know Zoey was into the drug scene on the island. They either knew something they shouldn't have known, or they crossed the wrong guy. I'm sure the sheriff's department…with the help of Seattle Homicide will figure it out."

Jed snorted. "You have a lot more faith in the Dead Falls Sheriff's Department than I do."

"I did throw Seattle PD in there. I'm sure they see these types of crimes all the time." She rubbed her palms against the thighs of her jeans. "I'd better get inside. If Stephanie's daughter was home at the time of the murder, I may have another little patient to see."

"So sad for those kids." He opened his door. "I'll walk you up to your porch. Aren't you glad I waited now?"

"I'm sure I don't have anything to worry about." But she

was glad. The mansion, as Jed called it, sat in an area of the island where each house had acreage. Her nearest neighbor lived a few miles away. Nobody would hear her scream out here—not that she planned on screaming.

Jed's shoulder bumped hers as they walked up to the wide veranda that almost encircled the house. She'd be fine as long as he didn't take her hand again. She'd almost gone weak in the knees when he'd grasped her hand by the swing set. She'd never been able to resist him, and a stint in prison and a surly demeanor hadn't changed that.

He waited until she inserted the key in the lock, and then touched her shoulder. "I hope you don't have a new patient tomorrow. I hope that little girl was nowhere near her mother at the time of her death."

"I hope so, too." She bumped the door with her hip. "Good night, Jed."

She closed the door and sensed his presence on the porch until she slid the dead bolt home. He really didn't have to worry about her, but his concern gave her the warm fuzzies. As much as he tried to push her away and play the tough guy, she knew the connection between them hadn't fizzled. That spark they'd first felt as kids running around the island still existed.

Except they weren't kids anymore, and Jed Swain had become a very complicated man—one she couldn't afford to sort out.

JED SAT OUTSIDE Hannah's house until she extinguished every light inside, except for a yellow glow from a small window on the landing. Most of the bedrooms in that behemoth of a house faced the back, with views of the woods and a peek of the bay.

The homes out here sat on acres of property, so Hannah's neighbors were few and far between. He didn't like it—not with a murderer loose on the island. Not that Hannah had anything to do with the drug culture on the island, but she saw patients, including Sheldon Grady, who did. What if someone wanted to find out what Sheldon knew about his mother's murder?

He groaned and smacked his palms on the steering wheel. Hannah Maddox had ceased to be his concern when her father had him shipped off to prison. Out of sight, out of mind.

If he'd had any sense at all, he would've stayed in LA or moved back to San Luis Obispo instead of trying to prove to the good citizens of Dead Falls Island that they'd been wrong about him. He'd soon come to the realization when he got here that he didn't give a damn what any one of them thought about him…until he ran into Hannah.

He started the car and pulled away from her house. On the way back to the Mitchells' place, he veered toward the shoulder of the road and looked up Stephanie's address—stored in an e-mail Michael had sent him. Hannah had just found out about the murder, so the cops would still be on the scene. If anyone else on the island knew about the crime, he wouldn't be the only one in the vicinity.

He didn't need to enter the address in his phone's GPS. He recognized Stephanie's address as the house where Michael had grown up. Michael's father had never remarried, so his wife must've retained some stake in the house or Michael had generously allowed his half sister to live there.

The house occupied a small lot on the edge of a subdivision off the main road that circled the island. At the turnoff for the community, Jed noticed more activity than usual for this time of night. Word of Stephanie's death must've gotten out already, and the late-night denizens of the island bars had flocked to the scene—easier for him to keep a low profile.

He circled around the edge of the homes, following the line of the park that the residents had demanded after the builder completed the construction. At the last turn to Stephanie's house, a police cruiser blocked the entrance to the street and a few clutches of people hovered at the scene.

Jed pulled over, well away from the cop car. He'd already had his encounter with the sheriffs tonight. Didn't need another one.

Hands in his pockets, he sauntered up to one group of people, their arms crossed and their heads together whispering. Their pajamas and robes marked them as the neighbors, as opposed to the bunch lounging near their cars in denim and leather.

He cleared his throat. "I heard Stephanie Boyd was murdered."

Four pale faces turned his way, and he recognized Karl Lundstrom and his wife. Karl had lived down the street from Michael's family back in the day.

"Oh, hey. That you, Jed?"

Jed stuck out his hand. "Yes, sir, Mr. Lundstrom."

"Call me Karl." He sliced a hand through the air. "Hadn't seen you since you've been back. Damn shame about what happened to you. Never believed it."

Then Karl had been in the minority. "Appreciate that."

"Now Zoey Grady is dead, along with this one." Karl gestured toward the flashing lights in front of Stephanie's house, the medical examiner's van parked at the curb.

His wife ducked her head and whispered, "Drugs…both of those girls."

Karl patted his wife's frail shoulder. "We don't know that yet, Charlene."

"Did any of the neighbors hear or see anything? Who discovered her body?" Jed kicked his toe against the curb.

The other woman in the group put her hand over her heart. "The little girl discovered her in the backyard."

Jed swallowed. Hannah would most likely have another patient. "That's messed up."

"She screamed and screamed." Charlene wiped a tear from her cheek. "Woke up the neighbors next door. I just can't believe it happened in this neighborhood. Zoey's place—well, that area is run-down."

"In the backyard." Another victim murdered outside her house, or incapacitated inside and dragged out. Jed rubbed his chin, then noticed four pairs of eyes watching him. He jerked his thumb over his shoulder. "I was just heading home. Stay safe."

He strode to his car, his spine straight, as he felt the neighbors' gazes drilling him between the shoulder blades. He blew out a breath when he got behind the wheel. Both murders might be tied to the drug trade in Discovery Bay, but the involvement of the children put Hannah right in the center of the maelstrom.

As he started his engine, his phone buzzed, and he plucked it out of his cup holder. The name on the display punched him in the gut. He closed his eyes and answered.

"Michael."

"Jed, I'm sorry to call you so late, but I just had some devastating news."

"I already know about Stephanie. I'm so sorry, man. And I'm sorry I never contacted her before…before…"

"The Dead Falls Sheriff's Department just notified me.

I couldn't believe it when they told me it looked like homicide. A drug overdose wouldn't have surprised me, but this?" Michael's voice broke on a sob.

"You still overseas?"

"Yeah, yeah." Michael sniffed.

"Let me know if there's anything I can do for you, Michael. I mean it this time."

"There is something you can do, Jed."

Jed squinted at the police activity beyond the barricade. "Yeah, anything, man."

"When I ran into you in LA, you mentioned that you had your PI license and had been doing some work for those attorneys who helped your case."

"That's right."

Michael coughed. "I mean, that's why I asked you to look into Stephanie's activities, you know? Well, that and being a Dead Falls native."

"Yeah?"

"And I wouldn't ask this, but you know better than anyone how corrupt and useless the sheriff's department is."

"Yeah?" A pulse in Jed's temple had started throbbing. "What is it, Michael? What do you want me to do?"

"Dude, I need you to investigate my sister's murder."

Chapter Six

Siggy woke her up early with a paw to the face. Hannah pulled the cat close and kissed the top of his head, his fur tickling her lips. "I see you, boy."

He squirmed in her arms and jumped from the bed; mission accomplished. Hannah snagged her phone from the charger and scrolled through her texts. She tapped on the one from Maggie, asking her if she'd heard about the Boyd murder.

News traveled fast in a small town, and the island functioned just like a small town—one surrounded by water, with ferries, plenty of gossip, old families, newbies—and now murder.

She texted Maggie back, letting her know she knew about the murder and inquiring about Sheldon. She watched for a few minutes for a response, and then rolled out of bed. If she didn't get up now, Siggy would be back with a second attempt.

She had to secure a set of wheels for the day, with two patients to see this morning and an afternoon meeting with Sheldon, if Maggie approved. She hoped to get Sheldon here at her office where she had a kids' room, fully stocked with toys and art supplies all designed to make children feel comfortable and safe.

When her mother announced she was done with the island and the house, Hannah had moved in and taken over, which included converting a small guesthouse on the property into an office. She saw most of her patients steps from her home.

That meant her patients knew where she lived, which could pose problems, but she hadn't had a serious issue yet. Especially as she treated mostly children, though she wouldn't have enough business on the island if she saw only children, so she did accept adults.

She'd flirted briefly with the idea of working with the prison population and had done some internship work at a women's penitentiary, but it had proved to be too painful. And after all that, Jed hadn't even tried to find out why she hadn't written to him. If it bothered him so much, he should've reached out to her.

Cupping her mug of steaming coffee, she stared out the kitchen window to the forest view. What had happened to all her letters?

Her gaze shifted to the pantry. Sheldon's runaway attempt had interrupted her thorough review of that box, but she had every intention of returning to the task in the hopes of unearthing information and maybe more boxes. She could just about believe her father had sabotaged her correspondence to Jed, but to set him up? Could he have been that evil?

She slurped some hot coffee as Siggy wrapped around her ankles. There was no shortage of evil on the island. No shortage of secrets, either. She'd had no idea Stephanie Boyd was related to Michael.

When her phone rang, she snatched it from the counter. "Hey, Maggie."

Maggie dispensed with the small talk again. "Can you believe there's been another murder? What the hell is going on?"

"Have you heard any more details?" Hannah nudged Siggy with her foot to shuffle to the breakfast nook. "The news I got last night was bare bones. I know she had a daughter."

"Yeah, get ready. Law enforcement wants us involved again."

Hannah sank to a chair, clutching her mug. "Did the child witness anything?"

"They don't know yet, but this Seattle cop wants you to talk to Stephanie Boyd's daughter." Maggie swore. "And I've got another one in the system."

Hannah said, "I understand Stephanie has a half brother. Any other relatives who can take the daughter?"

"Mother somewhere, but she's unavailable at the moment."

"Unavailable?" Hannah took another sip of coffee. "Unless she's locked up, what would keep a grandmother from her granddaughter after her own daughter had been murdered?"

"I don't have the details yet. The uncle is out of the country for work." Maggie took a deep breath. "What's your opinion? Do you think they're linked?"

"Both Zoey and Stephanie had drug problems. Maybe they pissed off the wrong person."

"Could be, but both single moms? Is that just a coincidence?"

Hannah chewed on her bottom lip, thinking about Astrid Mitchell and her son. "I think it's more telling that they were both heavy into the drug culture."

"You're probably right."

"How's Sheldon this morning?"

"He's okay. Slept late. Pancakes for breakfast. Still wants to go back to the house, but I don't think that's a good idea. Do you think you can get the keys from the sheriff's department and swing by Zoey's place to get this toy?"

Hannah ran a fingertip along the rim of her cup. "Do you believe there's a treasured toy he forgot?"

"Not really, but we'll make the effort. He says it's a set of magnetic train cars."

"I'll do it. Am I still on to see him this afternoon?"

"Ah, I was going to tell you. Will tomorrow work? He has a doctor's appointment later today. The doc squeezed him in."

"Tomorrow is fine. Better. I need to get my car today."

Maggie cleared her throat. "How's your…friend?"

"Jed?" Siggy had flopped at her feet and was now licking Hannah's toes in a new ploy for food. "He's all right. Felt bad about Sheldon's accusation but wasn't surprised Zoey had been bad-talking him to her son. Zoey was unhinged."

"He's lucky he had an alibi…and for this one."

A flare of anger leapt in Hannah's chest, and she pressed one palm against the table. "I guess people are quick to point the finger at the ex-con, but Jed never belonged in prison in the first place."

"Yeah, I heard the story. Read about his story before I even came to the island. Bad break. Look, I gotta go. Just wanted to give you a heads-up about Stephanie's daughter."

"What's her name?"

"Chrissy."

"Thanks, Maggie."

When Hannah ended the call, she made another to Jimmy

at the auto shop. He assured her he'd deliver her car this afternoon and send a tow to the Mitchells' place to get her old truck.

Feeling back in business, she fed Siggy and made some breakfast for herself. As she spooned her oatmeal into her mouth, she flipped open her laptop and clicked on articles about Stephanie's murder.

It didn't take her long to work her way through most of the information, as the cops were being tight-lipped about the case. No cause of death. No clues. No motive. The only thing she got out of the online articles was that the body was discovered outside…just like Zoey's.

The cops wouldn't make any connections between the two cases publicly, but the true crime chat rooms and murder blogs weren't holding back. Speculation was always easy.

When she glanced at the time, she scooted back her chair, startling Siggy, who flicked his tail at her while giving her a dirty look.

Although her session with Sheldon had been canceled for the day, she had other clients to see.

She'd been concerned she wouldn't be able to concentrate during the sessions with everything else going on, but as always, her patients' lives sucked her in, and she managed to be present for both of them.

When her last patient left, Hannah changed clothes and decided to tackle the attic again. She'd rescued the one box that contained Jed's case, but she'd seen a few others of interest up there. She may have been able to put her own issues on hold, but that didn't mean she'd forgotten about them.

She tugged on the rope for the attic door, a proper flashlight clutched in her other hand this time. Siggy scrambled from wherever he was napping and joined her at the foot of the ladder.

Crouching down, she scratched him beneath the chin. "Now I know how to get you to come running."

She climbed the ladder and flicked on the flashlight as she stepped into the space. She almost tripped over one of the boxes she'd dragged out the night before—the box containing her father's possessions from the job. This box had been on top of the August box and appeared to be in the same condition as the other one.

She flipped off the lid and aimed the beam of light inside the box. A few plaques on top trapped the papers and folders beneath them. She lifted the plaques and put them on the floor.

She thumbed through the file folders, holding her breath, but if she expected to find anything related to Jed's case here, she'd walk away disappointed. She shoved the box to the entrance to the attic, anyway. She might as well do a little cleaning while she was up here and get rid of some of this stuff. Mom wouldn't want it.

She crawled on her hands and knees through the dust to another box sporting her father's bold handwriting. She lifted one corner of the lid and peered inside, the light from her flashlight skimming over what looked like the contents of an office desk—paperclip holder, sticky notes, random little keys, a few old floppy disks and a thumb drive.

She grabbed a plastic bag crumpled in one corner of the box, shook it out and stuffed the disks, drive and keys into it. Then she secured the lid back onto the box and shoved it next to the other one. She didn't want to maneuver the heavy boxes down the ladder by herself, so she left them in the attic as she backed out, flashlight in hand, plastic bag dangling from her wrist. She could retrieve them later.

She stopped halfway down and called Siggy. He gave her a muffled mew and she took one step back up to peer into the attic, spotting his golden eyes gleaming in the darkness.

"You don't want to be trapped in there. Trust me." She tried calling "kitty, kitty" but Siggy had bigger fish to fry up there.

She dropped the bag on the kitchen table, washed her hands at the sink and then cracked open the tab on a can of cat food. That had Siggy purring at her ankles within seconds.

She scooped a spoonful of food into his bowl and secured the attic while he gobbled his grub.

Hannah toyed with one of the floppy disks at the table, wondering how she could view the contents. There had to be places that converted data from a floppy to a digital file. She didn't exactly know what she expected to find among her father's old stuff, but Jed's accusation had struck some chord with her—not that she'd admit that to him yet.

She checked her phone, but nobody was coughing up any more details about Stephanie's murder. As she had to drop by the station to pick up the keys to Zoey's place, she'd snoop around to see what she could find out about this new murder.

She showered, scrubbing the dust and grime from the attic off her body, and dressed down in jeans and a T-shirt. Although summer was still on the books, fall hovered on the edges, making its presence known when the sun set, so she grabbed a sweater and stuffed it into her oversize bag. She planned to pick up Sheldon's toy, but you never knew what you might find at a murder scene.

When she reached the sheriff's station, she landed in the middle of a hub of activity. Seattle PD had moved in with a vengeance and had claimed one of the conference rooms in the small station. It didn't look like too many Dead Falls deputies were welcome in that room. This already had all the earmarks of a circus.

She leaned over the front desk and snapped her fingers to get the desk sergeant's attention. "Hey, I'm here for the keys to Zoey Grady's house."

That got her noticed. His head jerked up, and he dropped the paper he'd been studying. "What's that? The Grady house?"

"I'm Dr. Hannah Maddox." She held a PhD, not an MD, and rarely used the doctor in front of her name, but sometimes it opened doors. "I'm treating Sheldon Grady, and he needs something from the house."

"Oh, right, right." The sergeant repeated her gesture and snapped at a passing patrol woman, getting a withering look in return. "Amanda, can you *please* get Dr. Maddox the keys to the Grady place?"

"Of course, Sarge." Amanda winked at Hannah and disappeared in the back, where the noise level had seemed to increase during the few minutes Hannah had been standing there.

Hannah backed away from the front desk and claimed a chair in the corner, sinking into its cushions. She buried her face in her phone and didn't make a move when Amanda returned, Zoey's key chain dangling from her fingers.

Amanda came out from the front desk area and jingled the keys a little to get Hannah's attention, even though the officer already had it.

Hannah slowly raised her eyes from her phone, her fingers still typing gibberish to no one. "Oh, thanks. Can you sit for a few seconds? I'm communicating with the social worker."

Amanda perched on the edge of the chair next to her. "Poor kid…and this one, too."

Hannah finally stopped typing and stuffed the phone into her purse. "I know. It's tragic for these kids. I haven't heard much about the Boyd case but if I'm going to be working with little Chrissy, I'm assuming she's a witness."

Amanda's eyes widened and she threw a glance at the sergeant, still preoccupied with his paperwork. "I'm not sure about that, but the Seattle gang is looking at the same killer for both. Same type of knife used in both murders. Both women dragged or chased from their homes and killed outside."

Hannah nodded, her heart thumping. "That's what I heard. To get the women outside, maybe the killer threatened to harm the kids. He probably wanted to kill them outside to avoid waking up the kids."

"But we still don't know if the kids did wake up. That's what you're going to find out, right?"

The sergeant called from the front desk. "Officer Robard, the Seattle crew needs some file."

Amanda muttered under her breath. "I've just about had it with the Seattle crew, and they haven't even been here two full days yet."

"If they have you fetching and serving, that's a good thing. You can get in and out of their war room and pick up some information."

"Not a bad plan." Amanda dropped the keys into Hannah's outstretched hand. "Good luck with those kids."

Hannah thanked her and left the station in her newly-serviced car. When she arrived at Zoey's trailer, the yellow crime scene tape hadn't budged. The investigators might just pay this house another visit to compare notes with Stephanie's place. But right now, Hannah had the place to herself.

She avoided the swing set, bloodstained rock and the dead bird and headed straight for the front door. The key from the key chain slid into the lock on the door handle and fit the dead bolt above it. Didn't look like any forced entry from this side. Had Zoey known her killer? Could've been her dealer—the same dealer Stephanie used. Could've been her ex, Chase.

Holding her breath, Hannah stepped over the threshold of the small house. When she had known Zoey, she'd lived in this same place with her parents, but her parents had kept a nicer home. As far as Hannah knew, Zoey's parents had turned this place over to Zoey and left the island. Hannah didn't know how Zoey had wound up in so much trouble, but she'd changed even before the birth of Sheldon, when Hannah had been away at college.

Trash, food containers, bottles, ashtrays and general disorder overwhelmed the small space of the living room—and all this occurred before the cops did their thing after the murder. Zoey's mother would have a heart attack if she could see her neat home now. Black fingerprint dust marked the door and windows, and the cops had tossed cushions and cut sections from the dirty carpet.

How had her friend from high school gotten to this point? Hannah remembered a girl interested in science, thinking about nursing school or even med school. Sitting on the arm of the threadbare couch, she leaned forward and stirred the contents of an ashtray with her fingertip.

The dregs of a few joints disintegrated beneath her touch,

and she dragged her black-tipped finger across an unused napkin from the pizza place lodged in a corner of a cushion. Drugs. That's how Zoey had gotten here. Was that what led to her murder?

She pushed up from the couch and headed toward the two bedrooms in the back of the house. She stumbled on more chaos but couldn't tell if the police or Zoey herself had caused it.

When she stepped into Sheldon's room, tears pricked the backs of her eyes. Why didn't Child Protective Services get involved here before Zoey's death? No child deserved to live like this. Where were Zoey's parents?

She plucked at the filthy sheets of the unmade bed and peered through the cracked window at the swing set. If Sheldon had been awake during his mother's murder and had been looking out this window, he would've seen it.

She turned her back on the scene and scanned the floor for the toy Sheldon had requested: a wooden train set, the cars connecting to each other with little magnets. She spotted one car on the chest of drawers, another on its side under the bed and the third in a cardboard box that functioned as a makeshift toy chest.

Hardly how a child would store a prized possession he couldn't live without, which confirmed her suspicion that he'd used it as an excuse to return to this dilapidated place—the only home he knew.

She sniffed and dropped the train cars in her bag as she picked her way across the floor. She'd already spent too much time in this house and stepping outside into the dusk gave her a chill.

She pulled the door closed and locked it. Pocketing the key chain, she strode to her car, her gaze flicking toward the swing set once. Behind the wheel of her car, she let out a long breath. Crime scenes definitely had a creep factor, especially with the yellow caution tape getting more bedraggled by the day.

On her way back to the station, she realized she'd be passing by another crime scene. Someone discovered Stephanie Boyd's body last night, so the investigators should be done with the site by now, but they'd leave the crime scene tape there until they were done processing. If they figured they had more forensics to collect, they'd be back.

However it still didn't prevent her from rubbernecking like half of the other residents of this island. She stepped on it and made the turn to Stephanie's property.

This well-ordered subdivision hardly looked like the scene of a drug murder, but that was the insidiousness of addiction—it struck across all socioeconomic classes.

She'd vaguely remembered the Ramsey family living in this middle-class enclave. Stephanie's half brother must've allowed her to stay in his father's home. Hannah had no idea whether Michael's father was still alive.

She parked on the side of the house, out of sight of the other residences as Stephanie's place hugged the edge of the community. She glanced at the forest to her right as she exited the car.

The trailer park where Zoey's house occupied had been more isolated than this development, but the forest hovered outside her doorway, too. Was location and convenience driving this killer?

She clicked her door and crept around to the front of house, still crisscrossed by yellow crime scene tape. A uniformed deputy lounged on the front porch, checking his phone, and she recognized Deputy Hill from the hospital when she'd questioned Sheldon. The investigators must think they still had evidence to process. Maybe they were still inside.

The neighbors and curiosity hounds had moved on—for now. Darkness had settled on the subdivision, bringing with it a cool mist, a sure sign that summer was waning.

Hill wouldn't let her inside, but she might be able to wrestle a few nuggets of info from him. She squared her shoulders and marched up to the house.

"Hi, Deputy Hill."

His gaze shot up from his phone, as he bobbled it. "Oh, hello, Dr...."

"Maddox, but you can call me Hannah." She gestured toward the front door, firmly closed. "Did the ME take the body?"

He glanced over his shoulder and licked his lips. "A long time ago."

"Did the investigators gather much evidence from the house?" She shoved one hand in the front pocket of her jeans and toyed with the keys to Zoey's house.

"Um, they're still working in there, Dr.—Hannah. It's the squad from Seattle. They don't tell me much of anything."

"I understand. The big boys...and girls move in and muscle out the local PD. Familiar story." She leaned in and whispered, "I'm going to be working with Stephanie's daughter, so they must believe there's a connection between the two murders. Do you know what they have?"

He whipped his head back and forth. "Not a thing. No."

"Okay, but if you hear anything that's not public knowledge, maybe you could fill me in. I need all the help I can get if I'm going to help that little girl, and I'm not sure the Seattle PD cares much about that. You know—" she stuck up her index and middle fingers together "—us locals have to stick together."

"Oh, yeah, sure." Hill reddened to the roots of his fair hair.

She dug one of her business cards from her purse and tucked it into the chest pocket of his khaki uniform shirt and patted it. "I appreciate it."

Before he could protest, she twirled around on the porch and scurried down the front walkway. She didn't want Seattle Homicide to find her out here snooping around.

She turned the corner and pressed the key fob to unlock her car. As she grabbed the door handle, dried leaves and twigs from the forest floor crackled behind her.

She spun around, clutching her keys between her fingers like jagged teeth.

Jed held up his hands as he emerged from the trees. "It's just me."

She sagged against her car. "You scared me. What are you doing out here?"

"I'm working for Michael Ramsey. He asked me to investigate his sister's murder." He put a finger to his lips.

Hannah's mouth dropped open. "You're kidding."

"Nope. I told you I had my PI license in California, and I did the paperwork when I got to Washington to transfer it here—just in case."

"Just in case you were going to be skulking around investigating a murder?" She took in his black jeans and T-shirt, noting the way it hugged his chest beneath the open hoodie. He'd obviously engaged in the time-honored tradition of most prison inmates—working out with weights in the yard.

She gritted her teeth against the bile that rose in her throat every time she thought about Jed incarcerated.

"Just in case I needed to pick up some work while I'm waiting for the academy to start." He shrugged. "But I'm doing this gratis. I owe Michael. I should've visited his sister as soon as I got here. Maybe I could've prevented her murder."

"I doubt that." She scooped back her hair and held it in a ponytail over her shoulder. "How does that work exactly? You march up to Seattle Homicide and tell them you're working the case?"

He snorted. "It's not that easy, but I did do a little searching of the grounds before they chased me off. And I found something."

She widened her eyes as a trill of adrenaline zigzagged up her spine. "What did you find?"

He plunged his hand into the pocket of his hoodie, and a plastic bag crinkled as he pulled it out. He dangled it in front of her.

"I found a dead bird near where Stephanie's body was discovered."

Chapter Seven

Hannah's wide eyes swung back and forth as they followed the sway of the bag between his fingers. In a breathless voice, she said, "Another dead bird."

"Yeah, odd, huh?" He carefully placed the bag back in his pocket.

"D-did you tell the detectives?"

"They didn't give me a chance." He raised one shoulder. "They chased me off before I could tell them what I found. It's not like the bird wasn't there when they canvassed the area. Unless someone moved it over there, the condition of the bird indicates to me that it had been there at least a few hours. They either missed it or didn't think it was important."

Hannah wound her hair around her hand. "They didn't bag the bird from the scene of Zoey's murder, either. But you'd think a second dead bird might trigger something."

"You'd think." He scratched his chin. "I have a feeling the cops are already getting tunnel vision on this one. Both women used drugs, had contact with local drug dealers and ran with a druggie crowd. I know they're questioning Chase Thompson, but I think they're gonna start looking hard at the island trade, round up the usual suspects and do a full-court press."

Hannah screwed up one side of her mouth in a gesture reminiscent of their time in chemistry class when she was trying to figure out the valence of an element. "Why would a drug dealer leave a dead bird at the scene of a hit? As far as I know, cartels don't have mascots. And if they do, I doubt it's a cute little bird."

"Maybe the cops have more evidence of a drug hit than they've let on. They probably assumed the bird was part of the landscape. It's not like the poor little guys are out of place. They're part of this forest ecosystem and death is a part of that ecosystem."

"It's part of ours, too." She rubbed her palms against the thighs of her jeans, which fit her just right. "What now?"

"How about dinner?" He regretted the words as soon as they left his lips. It was those damned tight jeans hugging Hannah's...curves.

He held his breath, bracing for a refusal. He'd been trying his best to push her away, so he didn't deserve her acceptance...even though he wanted it.

"Dinner." She cocked her head. "You're giving me whiplash here, Swain."

"I just thought you might be able to help me on the case. God knows, I'm not gonna get much from the cops, and you're responsible for the kids." She opened her mouth, and he thrust out his hands, palms first. "Not that I expect you to tell me anything the kids say, but you do have connections in the sheriff's department. Connections I can use."

She lifted her dark eyebrows in a perfect arch. "So, this is a working dinner?"

"Sort of. I'll buy."

"Not necessary." She flicked her fingers, and his heart sank. "I put some chicken in the fridge to defrost, and now I'm going to have to eat it. You can help me."

He swallowed. "I don't want you going to any trouble."

"Who said I'm going to any trouble? Especially for a work dinner." She opened her car door. "Follow me home."

"Yes, ma'am." He put his fingers to his forehead as she slammed her door and punched on her engine.

He watched her taillights disappear, and then jogged to his truck, which he'd parked outside the subdivision. He hadn't given dinner a thought until he blurted out his invitation, but brainstorming with Hannah might be just what he needed to kick-start this investigation. He didn't want to fail Michael again.

By the time he arrived at Hannah's house, the oven was already preheating and she had poured two glasses of iced tea. He didn't drink alcohol, but he didn't care if others drank in his presence. He never considered himself an alcoholic, but his father had covered that ground thoroughly and Jed didn't want to tempt his genetic makeup. He not only had his own family as evidence, but half the guys in prison were there because of issues caused by substance abuse. He'd had enough problems in his life. He didn't need to invite more.

On his way to the kitchen, he shrugged out of his hoodie and hung it on the back of an ornately carved dining room chair, the baggie with the dead bird crinkling in his pocket. The dark dining room and empty table, polished to a glistening sheen, signaled they'd be eating in the cozier breakfast nook in the kitchen. That suited him much better.

He nearly jumped out of his skin when a cat wound itself around his ankles and meowed. He bent forward and scratched under its chin. He called out. "Is this cat going to go for the bird in my pocket?"

"Siggy? He's only interested in live birds."

He whispered to the cat, "Siggy, huh? I'll bet your full name is Sigmund Freud, but I won't tell anyone."

He joined Hannah in the kitchen and washed his hands, and then he picked up his glass and clinked it with hers. "Have some wine or a beer, if you want."

"I want to be alert for this discussion." She tapped her fingernail against her glass. "I wasn't kidding about a low-key dinner. I'm just going to dump some barbecue sauce from a jar over this chicken and stick it in the oven to bake. I've got some stuff for a salad, and I can pop some red potatoes in the microwave and toss them with a little butter and pepper."

"Sounds like haute cuisine to me." He reached for the fridge. "I'll make the salad."

They worked side by side in silence, Siggy making the rounds every few minutes to check on the chicken. This had been about the closest Jed had been to domesticity since the Law Project sprung him from the joint. He hadn't dated much since his release. Most women ghosted him once he told them about his past, and he didn't blame them. How could they be sure he hadn't really been guilty?

He stole a glance at Hannah's left ring finger as she used a spoon to spread the barbecue sauce over the chicken pieces. Astrid had been sure to tell him Hannah wasn't married or engaged. Had she ever worn a ring on that finger? Was there someone she still dreamed about at night like he dreamed of her?

She poked him in the back, and he almost sliced off the

tip of his finger. "If you chop those cucumbers any smaller, we'll be able to drink them."

He glanced at the cutting board, a warmth crawling across his skin. "I promised you a chopped salad, and I'm gonna deliver."

She giggled and placed the chicken in the oven, the glass baking dish clanging against the metal rack. "The chicken's going to take about forty-five minutes, but we can eat the salad while we talk about those birds."

"I can wait." Using the knife, he scraped the cucumbers from the cutting board into the salad bowl and held up a green pepper. "You want this in there?"

"Sure." She scooted around him and ducked into the fridge, emerging with a bottle of dressing in each hand. "I have Italian and ranch."

"Italian is fine."

She placed the bottle of salad dressing on the small table in the breakfast nook that looked out on the dark forest. No drapes or blinds covered the three-paned window, and his reflection stared back at him as he placed the salad bowl on the table.

"You ever consider covering some of these windows?" He pulled out a chair at the same time she placed a laptop next to the salad. She'd been dead serious about this being a working dinner.

Looking up, she squinted outside. "Window coverings distract from the view."

He scooped the salad into the two bowls she'd set on place mats covered in yellow sunflowers and grabbed the dressing. "I noticed you have a security system, though."

She sighed. "I don't think I have to worry about the same killer who's targeting Zoey and Stephanie, do you?"

"We don't know yet why those two women were killed, so yeah, you kinda do." He stabbed a multicolor selection of raw veggies with his fork and stuffed them in his mouth.

"Then let's get on that." She pulled the laptop toward her and brought up a search engine. With her fingers flying across the keyboard, she said, "I'm going to search for crime scenes and birds. Do you think that's a good place to start?"

"That's a general place to start." He pointed a fork at her bowl. "Your salad is going to get soggy."

"I can actually eat and type at the same time." She punched Enter on her keyboard and attacked her salad with as much gusto as the search engine returned a page of results.

He turned the computer toward him and scanned the results. "Not promising, although there are a lot of weird stories here. Try entering 'finches.'"

"Finches?" She dragged the yellow napkin from her lap and dabbed her lips. "That bird was a finch?"

He pulled the laptop toward him, nudging his bowl out of the way. "It's a house finch to be exact—a female. Males are prettier."

Bumping his elbow with hers, she said, "Both of those birds were finches?"

"Both female finches and both dead."

"That's not a coincidence, Jed." She rubbed her arms and hopped up from her chair. "I'll rinse off those potatoes and stick them in the microwave."

He did a search for house finches in Washington State while Hannah ran the water in the sink and Siggy weaved around her ankles. The microwave beeped as she set the timer for the potatoes. Then she walked back to the table and hung over his shoulder, the tip of her ponytail tickling his neck.

"Find anything interesting about our finches?"

Jabbing his finger at the screen, he said, "Their scientific name is *Haemorhous mexicanus*, they're native to western North America and commonly kept as pets."

"I wonder if Zoey or Stephanie had any pet birds. I don't remember seeing any birdcages in Zoey's place." Hannah perched on the edge of her chair, clasping her hands between her knees.

Jed jerked his head up. "You were in Zoey's house? Before her murder?"

"After. Remember last night when Sheldon said he'd gone home to get a toy? I was allowed to collect the keys to Zoey's house to retrieve that toy."

"Do you still have the keys to Zoey's house?"

She clapped a hand over her mouth. "As a matter of fact, I do. I was on my way to the sheriff's station to return them when I made that detour to Stephanie's house."

He nodded, storing that information away for later. "Okay."

"I don't like that look on your face." She narrowed her eyes. "What are you thinking?"

"Stephanie's and Zoey's murders are related. Stephanie's brother asked me to do some nosing around, and you have the keys to the first victim's house. What do you think?"

"If anyone finds out I let you into Zoey's house, the sheriff's department may never trust me again."

"Let me in?" He widened his eyes. "It wouldn't be your fault if I lifted the keys from…"

"They're in my purse."

He nodded. "…your purse and let myself in."

"You're sneaky." She smacked him on top of the head with a square pot holder.

As the timer beeped on the microwave, he held up a finger. "Saved by the bell."

They spent the next fifteen minutes eating the baked chicken and potatoes, which Hannah had dismissed as basic, but tasted like heaven to him. He enjoyed the food, but he enjoyed the company more, even the cat rubbing its head against his shins.

When he finished, Jed pushed away his plate and pinched a little piece of chicken between his fingers. He held it out to Siggy, who snapped it between his teeth.

"Whoa, he's a tiger." Jed wiped his fingers on the napkin, glancing at Hannah's pursed lips. "What? He's not allowed to have chicken?"

"Not from the table. It raises his expectations and teaches him bad habits."

"That's what I do best." He waved the napkin over the table. "Let me clean up, and you can take the laptop and look into finches some more. Maybe there's some weird symbolism to them."

"You got a deal." She swept the computer from the table. "If you don't mind, I'll have that glass of wine now."

"Go sit down. I'll bring it to you." He pushed away from the table and stacked some dishes. He dumped them into the sink, cleared the rest of the table and yanked open the fridge door, calling over his shoulder. "Do you want white, and do you have any open?"

"Yes, and yes. Top shelf, open bottle of chardonnay."

He grabbed the bottle by the neck and thumbed off the rubber stopper Hannah had inserted. He poured the golden liquid into a wineglass and swirled it. It caught the light, winking at him, as he carried it out to Hannah. The stuff didn't even tempt him.

He placed it on the coaster at her elbow. "Find anything interesting?"

"Nope." She picked up the glass and took a sip. "You can just leave the dishes if you want."

"No way. Keep looking."

He returned to the kitchen, loaded the dishwasher and tipped a bottle of soap over the greasy baking pan. One blue bubble formed at the tip. "Hannah, you're out of dishwashing liquid. Any under the sink?"

"There's a new bottle in the pantry—to your left when you open the door."

He remembered where the pantry was located. In his younger years, the pantry in the Maddox house had intrigued him—not just cupboards for food but a whole room for it.

He pulled open the door to the pantry and flicked on the light. Turning slightly to the left, he tripped over a box on the floor. A flurry of dust made him sneeze.

He leaned forward to shove the box out of the way, and a scribble of black writing caught his attention. The date on the box was seared into his soul, and he dropped to a crouch.

Why was Hannah looking into his case?

Chapter Eight

Hannah frowned at the pictures of the finches and took another sip of wine. Why were the males of the species always so much more flamboyant than the females? Show-offs.

She cocked her head. Jed had stopped clanking pots and pans in the kitchen. "Did you find the dishwashing liquid in the pantry?"

He appeared before her on silent feet, a dark cloud marring his features. "I got sidetracked."

"Sidetracked?" She wrinkled her nose. Jed always did have a fascination for that pantry.

"Yeah, I tripped over the box containing files about my case."

Her heart skipped in her chest, and she put one hand over it. "I—I can explain that."

His jaw tight, Jed crossed his arms. If a face ever personified, "I'm waiting and I won't believe you, anyway," Jed's had it down.

"Sit down." She shoved the computer from her lap and patted the cushion next to her. "Please."

He rolled his broad shoulders and took the seat next to her on the couch, his weight causing her to tip to the side, her shoulder tapping his. He shifted away from her.

"I wasn't checking up on you or trying to verify the evidence that cleared you."

"Or looking for clues that would tie me to Zoey's murder?"

She whipped her head back and forth, her ponytail lashing the side of her face. "Don't be absurd. I, and everyone else, know you had nothing to do with Zoey's murder...or Stephanie's."

"Thanks for throwing Stephanie in there, too." The corner of his eye twitched.

"When we were at the Mitchells' you accused my father of setting you up for Zoey's rape." She scooped in a deep breath. "It got me thinking. I knew he kept notes on cases at home, and I wondered if he'd kept anything about yours that would implicate him."

He rubbed at the twitch. "Why would he do that? He'd want to destroy any evidence, not enshrine it in a memory book."

"You didn't know my father."

"Maybe if I had known him better, I never would've allowed myself to fall into his trap. I realized he didn't approve of the two of us getting closer, but I never imagined in my wildest dreams that he'd go so far as to set me up for a crime. Once I was serving my sentence, I had a lot of time to think and piece things together." He smacked his hand on the arm of the couch. "That's when I figured out what he'd done."

"But what did he do and why?" She held up her hands. "I know you believe he did it to break us up, but he could've achieved that a number of ways. Trust me. He still held the purse strings. He could've threatened to cut me off, not pay my college tuition, taken away my car." She lifted one shoulder. "I wasn't very strong back then. We'd had a long friendship but had just started getting romantic."

"So, you would've taken the car over me?"

She searched his face for a telltale sign of humor—the raised eyebrow, the quirk in his lips—nothing.

She cleared her throat. "I'm just saying, my dad ruled the house. My mom never said one word against him, totally did his bidding."

"Like pretending to mail your letters to me?"

"Exactly." She brushed her hands together. "But back to the point. My father didn't need to send you to prison to keep us apart. If he did set you up, and I'm not disagreeing that's a possibility, he must've had another reason. You didn't have anything on him, did you?"

"Me?" He poked himself in the chest. "Dumb kid from the wrong side of the falls? If I did have anything on the sheriff, I would've used it. I didn't know a thing about your father—except that he didn't much like me."

"Okay, that's why I went into the attic to snoop around. As I pointed out before, you didn't know my father. He held on to everything related to work." She pointed at the ceiling. "That's why he has those boxes up there. All his case files would be at the station and all digitized by now. He had no reason to save boxes of stuff from work, but he did."

"You think he went up there and caressed his files or something?"

"Ugh. Don't put that image in my head." She stuck out her tongue. "He had a huge ego. If he pulled off something like setting you up for a crime, he'd want to hold on to that proof."

"Sort of like a serial killer hanging on to trophies?"

"You're determined to give me nightmares about my father, aren't you?" She trailed her fingers down Jed's forearm, corded with veins and muscle. "Do you believe me? That I didn't have some nefarious reason for snagging that box from the attic?"

He glanced down at her fingers and ran a hand through his dark hair. "Just gave me an unwelcome shock when I saw it in the pantry. I thought you were...investigating me."

"I don't need to investigate you, Jed Swain." Her eyelashes fluttered beneath the intense stare from his dark eyes. "I know you inside and out."

Weaving his fingers into her hair, he cupped the back of her head and landed a savage kiss on her mouth. "Don't be so sure of that, Hannah. You knew a boy, and now I'm a man—an ex-con."

She put her fingers to her throbbing lips as tears pricked the backs of her eyes. "Don't call yourself that. You didn't do anything wrong. You never should've been in prison, and now everyone knows that."

He released her, the fire dying from his eyes as a sad smile played across his mouth. "Doesn't alter the fact that I did time. That changes a man."

She caught her bottom lip between her teeth. Who was she to argue with him? He may have changed, but that kiss proved the chemistry between them still sizzled.

Bracing his hands on his knees, he pushed up from the couch. "Did you find anything?"

"In the box?" She tucked a strand of hair behind her ear that Jed had loosened from her ponytail. "I haven't had a chance to look yet."

"I meant on the finches." He strolled into the kitchen and started running water in the sink.

Her mouth gaped open for a second. He wasn't interested in what she discovered about her father or his case?

Clutching her empty wineglass, she followed him into the kitchen. She sidled next to him at the sink and rinsed out her glass. "You're not curious about what's in the box?"

Jed swirled the suds in the baking pan with the dish sponge and seemed mesmerized by the little whirlpool he'd created. Then he dumped the water down the drain. "I don't know if I want to find out how he did it or even why. It's enough that he ruined...no, interrupted my life. He didn't ruin it. I never gave him that satisfaction or power over me."

She bumped his hip with hers. "Well, I am curious, especially now that someone has murdered Zoey."

"What does Zoey's murder have to do with anything?" He rinsed the dish and reached across her for a dry towel.

"Just got me thinking about her. If my dad did set you up, he had to have been doing so with Zoey's knowledge or approval. Zoey knew damned well you didn't rape her. If my father tweaked some evidence or planted something, she would've known about it."

"Your father knew Zoey from her friendship with you, right?" Jed flicked the dish towel over his shoulder. "I can't imagine he'd let you hang out with someone without fully vetting her first."

Hannah rolled her eyes. "Zoey came over when my father was home. They exchanged casual conversation, just like any of my friends...just like with you."

He snorted. "My conversations with your father didn't fall into the category of casual. The man grilled me half the time."

"How come you never told me that?" She snatched the

towel from his shoulder and hung it on the oven handle. "I never heard him giving you the third degree."

"It didn't bother me, and I didn't want to bother you with it." He shook his head. "I never realized his suspicions of me would turn into a vendetta."

"I want to find out why." She jabbed her finger toward the pantry. "And I'm going to start with that box."

Hooking a thumb in his belt loop, he asked, "Are there more?"

"This box had the date of the crime on it. There was another box that contained supplies from his desk—maybe from when he retired. With everything that's been happening around here, I haven't had a chance to look through it." She nudged him. "Do you want to start now?"

"I thought we were supposed to be researching finches."

"We haven't had much luck with that, have we? I even tried 'symbolism of finches' and 'ceremonies with finches'—didn't find a thing."

His eyebrows shot up to his hairline. "Ceremonies with finches? I would hope you didn't find anything about that. That's just weird."

"I was desperate." She crooked her finger at him. "The box?"

"Okay." He yanked at the paper towel roll and tore off a length of paper. "Let's get some of that dust off first."

He followed her to the pantry, and she opened the door. He crouched beside the box and ran the paper towel over the lid and down the sides, picking up a gray film of dust. Then he wadded up the paper and hoisted the box in his arms. "Where to?"

"Put it on the coffee table in the family room." She scurried ahead of him. "I'll move my laptop over."

When she got to the family room, she shoved her laptop to one side of the coffee table and patted the gleaming wood surface. "Right here."

Jed lowered the box to the table and lifted the cardboard lid. Sitting on the edge of the couch, he peered into the box. "Files, papers, photos. This stuff isn't official, is it? Or copies of official case documents? He retired. He probably shouldn't have taken those."

"I have no idea. My father did what he wanted with that department." She sat beside him and dug into the box before lifting out a sheaf of papers.

Jed flipped open a file folder. "These are copies of the statements. This is Zoey's statement—her false statement."

She leaned over his arm and ran her finger down the page. She tapped some words highlighted in yellow. "What did he mark here?"

Jed squinted at the page. "The time of the so-called attack."

"She said it was between eleven and midnight."

He slid her a sideways glance. "You remember that?"

"I remember because you were at my place that night, and you left your wallet here." She swallowed a painful lump in her throat. "The wallet they never found at your house."

"Yeah, the wallet that was part of my alibi. I had driven to the all-night convenience store when I left your place but before I even walked inside, I realized I'd left my wallet at your house."

"You should've called me or driven back over. Then I could've been your alibi." She swiped the back of her hand across her tingling nose.

"Thank God you weren't dragged into it any more than you already had been." He flicked the edge of Zoey's statement with his finger. "If I hadn't left my wallet, I would've walked into that store, maybe talked to Jerry for a while. I would've bought my beer and had a receipt to prove my presence there. Instead, the camera on the parking lot wasn't working properly, and I didn't have any other way to prove I was there. Jerry never saw me drive up on the side of the store. Nobody walking in or out at the time."

"And then you drove to the falls by yourself." She gave a little shiver. So many innocent choices conspired against Jed that night. "And we never found your wallet. At least if the wallet had been at our house, that would've supported your explanation of why you didn't go inside the store."

"Yeah, my wallet conveniently disappeared from your house and turned up near Zoey's place."

"D-do you think my father had something to do with that, too?"

"Of course." His fingers dug into the paper underneath his hand, crinkling it. "Maybe that's why he circled the time of the assault on Zoey's statement—he needed to destroy my alibi."

Hannah put her hand to her mouth. "It's so diabolical, but I can't believe my father did all that just to keep us apart. Hell, we might've gone our separate ways when I returned to college in the fall, anyway."

"Do you believe that?" He smoothed the wrinkled piece of paper against the folder in his lap. "I don't know if I'd have ever let you go once you were mine."

Her breath caught in her throat. At that time, she'd already spent her freshman year away at college, dating other boys, even losing her virginity to someone else, but Jed had always been on her mind through it all.

She traced the tip of her finger along his bunched knuckles. "I guess we'll never know now."

His gaze dropped to her parted lips, but this time he blinked and flipped the folder shut. "I don't know that it matters now why he did it or even how. I'm sure he found my wallet at this house and planted it outside Zoey's house. That wasn't enough to convict me, but it didn't look good."

"I think I need to know."

"Maybe you do." He rubbed his eyes and dropped the folder into the box. "I need to know what happened to Michael's sister. Do you think you can use those keys and let me into Zoey's house?"

"Sure." She tossed a pen back into the box. She owed him that—and a lot more, if her father really did set him up. "I'm going to be pretty busy tomorrow. I have another appointment with Sheldon, and I may be talking to Stephanie's daughter, too."

"Sounds like a tough day." He rose to his feet and snagged his hoodie from the chair, then patted the pocket for the bagged bird. "If I get any more information from Michael about his sister, I'll let you know so you'll have some background dealing with Chrissy."

"I'd appreciate that." She circled the air over the box with her finger. "I'm still going to look through this box."

"You do that." Siggy had jumped up on the back of the couch, and Jed scratched behind his ear. "Sorry about the bird, buddy. Maybe I'll bring you something, next time, you can sink your claws into."

Hannah's mouth lifted on one side. At least it sounded like he'd be back—and he liked Siggy.

"I'll keep looking into the significance of finches." He shoved his arms into the hoodie. "Thanks for dinner."

She swept up Siggy as she walked Jed to the front door. She didn't want any awkwardness between them while saying goodbye. Would he kiss her? Did she expect him to? Did she even want him to? Siggy would function as a barrier between them.

Jed stepped onto the porch and stroked the pad of his thumb over the stripes on Siggy's head. "I'll update you if I discover anything, and if you're too busy tomorrow, I can take Zoey's keys and let myself in."

She smacked his upheld palm with her hand. "That would be a very bad idea, and you know it. I'm sure I can find some time tomorrow to go out there. My session with Sheldon might even warrant another visit—at least that's what I'll tell the sheriff's department when they ask me about the keys."

"That's a deal." He rubbed his hand on his thigh. "And, Hannah? Don't get too lost in that box."

She ducked her head. "Don't worry about it. I'll touch base with you tomorrow when I have a better idea of when I can go to Zoey's house."

He gave Siggy a final pat on the head, and then turned toward the long path and the driveway where he had parked his truck.

She watched him lope to his vehicle. He turned when he reached it and raised his hand.

She shut the door, leaned against it and sighed. Why couldn't things be easy with Jed anymore, like they used to be? She'd felt more comfortable with him than anyone else. That's when, after a year of college, she realized that what they shared could blossom into something more than a friendship.

He must've realized the same thing at the same time. The

heat between them positively sizzled that summer—and that's when the problems with Zoey started.

She pushed away from the door and obliged Siggy, twisting in her arms, by releasing him. He jumped onto the floor and sniffed under the kitchen table in the hopes she and Jed had dropped some food.

"Jed's already teaching you bad habits, isn't he? Don't think you're going to get table scraps from me at dinnertime."

Jed had done a good job cleaning the kitchen, leaving her nothing to do but hit the lights.

She threw a final glance at the box on the coffee table before going upstairs. She'd thought Jed would've shown more eagerness about going through those files. He was so confident in the truth about her father that he didn't need to see any proof. But she did.

She trudged up the steps to her bedroom. She didn't want to deal with it now. She had to prepare her office tomorrow for two lost, traumatized children.

She rushed through her bedtime routine, skipping the floss, and crawled between the covers and pulled her pillow in for a hug. What would it be like to sleep with Jed? They'd never gotten any further than a kiss—then or now. And the kiss he'd planted on her tonight was completely different from the shy, tentative smooches he'd teased her with many years ago. She tapped her bottom lip, which still buzzed with the sensation.

Siggy's mad dash into the bedroom and under her bed startled her out of her daydreams. Hannah leaned over the bed and lifted the bed skirt. Siggy's eyes glowed back at her in the dark.

"What is your problem?" Hannah scooted farther off the

bed and reached for the cat, her hand skimming over his quivering fur.

She flicked on the bedside lamp with unsteady fingers. The only thing that spooked Siggy like this was an unwelcome visitor.

Hannah swung her legs off the bed, her bare feet hitting the area rug that protected her from the cold hardwood. She said aloud for her benefit as well as Siggy's, "There can't be anyone inside the house. The alarm would've gone off."

She padded across the floor and stuck her head out the bedroom door, holding her breath. Only the sounds of the creaking house met her straining ears.

She crept downstairs, wishing she had one of her father's pistols locked and loaded in her hand. She'd left Siggy by the bay window in the family room that had a view of the front yard.

Kneeling on the window seat's cushion, she cupped her hand against the glass and peered outside, her breath fogging the window. She stared into the pitch black, and then pulled back with a gasp.

The porch light should be illuminating the scene. The bulbs over the driveway were connected to motion sensors, but the porch light stayed on all night. It had been on when she ushered Jed out the front door.

She tiptoed to the door and disabled the alarm. She unlocked it and eased it open.

Her heart slammed against her chest when she spied the broken glass from the bulbs that usually lit up the porch. But then it stopped cold when she saw the dead bird next to it.

Chapter Nine

Jed had spent the morning with Hannah at the sheriff's station, trying to convince them the two murders and the warning to Hannah were linked by the dead finches. He didn't want to do it, but in the end, he gave up the finch he'd found at Stephanie's house to the Seattle PD. At least they took him seriously now, but they weren't going to allow a PI to solve this case—especially a PI with a record, expunged or not.

His foot pressed against the accelerator, and his truck lurched forward. He needed to get to Hannah's house before Maggie delivered the first of her little patients. He didn't need a repeat of Sheldon's public assessment of his character.

He squeezed the steering wheel. How did Zoey end up hating him so much just because he never returned her interest? She'd never had a chance with him, and once Hannah had returned from her first year of college, any remote possibility that he and Zoey did have grew even more distant. As far as he remembered, he'd let Zoey down gently, never led her on and had even sent a few of his friends her way. What a mistake.

He'd learned later from his defense team that Zoey had had some mental health issues. Those issues had never come out in the trial. His lawyer at the time had wanted to play it safe and not dig into Zoey's personal life too deeply. Didn't want to blame the victim…except he's the one who was the victim.

He rolled into Hannah's driveway, pulling behind her car. Had the person who'd left the bird on her porch been watching him as he'd left her house last night? He hadn't seen any other cars on the road when he'd driven away, but then, he'd been distracted.

The forest ringing this house provided good cover for anyone wanting to do harm here. Her security system had been no help. After the stranger had broken the porch lights, he'd been able to creep up to the house from the forest side. Hannah's security footage showed a shadowy figure in indistinguishable black clothing, dark gloves and a hoodie, crouching down by her door and then slipping away. That person could've been anyone.

He parked and dragged the hardware store's plastic bag from the passenger seat. He noted the stepladder Hannah had left for him to reach the light fixtures above the high door. She'd already told him she'd be busy prepping the children's space in her office.

She'd called him first thing this morning, and he'd chided her for not contacting him when she'd found the bird last night. He had probably still been in his truck, driving back to the Mitchells', when she found the bird. He could've turned around right then, maybe giving him a chance to find the perpetrator.

She had called him even before she notified the police, though, and he'd had to convince her to do so. Now the birds had finally made it onto Seattle Homicide's radar.

He'd already talked to Michael about the finches, but Michael didn't have a clue. Said Stephanie would've been opposed to keeping birds in a cage and never would've owned them.

He grabbed the stepladder from where it leaned against the house and set it up on the porch. With gloved hands, he removed the broken stubs of the previous bulbs.

Hannah's security cam had caught something—most likely a rock thrown to break the bulbs—tripping the sensor lights seconds before it went dark. He hadn't found anything that fit the bill and neither had the police. The perp most likely took the object with him when he left or threw it into the forest. He might have been able to grab it when he crouched down to leave the dead bird on Hannah's welcome mat, as Siggy watched from the window.

Too bad the cat couldn't talk.

Jed unwrapped the new bulbs and screwed them into the sockets. He'd suggest that Hannah replace the fixtures with some that protected the bulbs so this couldn't happen again.

He hopped off the last rung of the ladder, his jaw clenched. It had better not happen again. What did this killer have to do with Hannah? He must know she was treating the kids. Did that mean the kids might be able to identify him?

If so, they were in more danger than Hannah.

"Thank you for doing that."

He cranked his head around to the sound of Hannah's voice, and she floated toward him, her long skirt swishing around her legs, her low-heeled shoes crunching the gravel that ringed the flower beds. She'd twisted her brown hair into a braid that hung over her shoulder. She could be some child's mom volunteering in the classroom. Must be a look she cultivated for the kids. He liked it.

"I was just thinking that you should get different fixtures." He pointed to the lights. "Something that protects the bulbs."

She squinted at the bulbs. "Maybe, but we both know nothing would've stopped my visitor last night. He was determined to leave that poor bird on my doorstep."

"He obviously wants the detectives to tie the crimes together. Was probably disappointed they hadn't done so already." Jed folded the stepladder and offered to carry it back to the toolshed.

Hannah led him around the side of the house to the landscaped backyard with its covered patio, gas grill and wet bar. Did Hannah entertain like her parents did? He'd spent several days over the summer months eating burgers and hot dogs and splashing in the pool with the rest of Hannah's friends from school. Her parents had always welcomed him—until his relationship with Hannah had made a turn toward the romantic.

He followed her to the toolshed at the edge of the property, near the line of the forest. A small creek bubbled beyond the lush lawn where the Maddoxes' hospitality had extended with Adirondack chairs placed in the water, so the adults could sip their alcoholic beverages while the kids frolicked in the water. Not that *his* parents were ever invited to a Maddox soiree.

"Earth to Jed." Hannah snapped her fingers. "You wanna take off your shoes, roll up your jeans and plant your feet in the creek?"

His gaze darted toward the door of the toolshed gaping open. "That does sound good about now, but I know you're expecting company."

"I am." She reached into the toolshed and tugged on the chain to illuminate the space. "You do know not to talk about the kids I'm seeing today, right? I really shouldn't have mentioned at all they that were my patients, but I figure everyone in town must know, anyway."

"Whoever left that bird knows." He hoisted the stepladder and carried it into the shed, which looked better than some houses on the island.

Twisting her fingers in front of her, she said, "Like I mentioned, everyone in town knows, so that doesn't narrow it down."

He swung the door of the shed closed and snapped the padlock on the outside. "At least it got the attention of the cops."

"I got the distinct impression they felt foolish after not taking you seriously when you found the second bird."

"Maybe, but that's not my intent." Jed clapped his hands together to dislodge dirt from his work gloves. "If they figure I'm trying to one-up them, they're not going to throw me any bones at all."

Hannah chewed on her bottom lip. "I might have a contact for you at the sheriff's department. I'll try to keep you in the loop."

"I don't need to figure out this thing on my own. I'd be happy to give them anything I find—like the bird. I just want to help Michael and get justice for those two women." *Even though Zoey had denied him justice.*

When they reached the front of the house, Jed collected the trash from installing the bulbs and tossed it into the back of his truck. He turned toward Hannah, who was on the porch. "We still on for tonight?"

"Tonight?" She shaded her eyes with her hand. "What's tonight?"

"Zoey's place. You do still have the keys, right? I didn't see you returning them this morning at the station."

"I forgot about the keys, and I don't remember making a date for that." She folded her arms, rocking back on her heels.

"We have one now. I'll even buy you dinner after." He ducked into his truck and started the engine without waiting for her answer. Her grin and shake of the head were answer enough.

It seemed as if Hannah couldn't resist him any more than he could her—even if it led them to disaster.

"FINCHES CAN MAKE good pets, as long as they're domesticated. They have a pretty song, too." Charlie pinged a cage with her finger, and the yellow bird within pinned her with his beady eyes.

Jed leaned against the counter of the pet shop, the chirping, rustling birds giving him a headache. "You don't recall anyone buying up finches recently, do you?"

"No." Charlie moved to the next cage and shoved a peanut through the mesh into the waiting claws of a hamster. "Finches are so common on the island, we don't even carry them in the store. Parakeets and cockatiels are more popular here. I'm sure you can find them in Seattle. Do you want the name of a store there?"

The last thing Jed wanted was a caged bird. He held out his hands. "No, I was just wondering if anyone on the island kept them."

"I'm sure they do." She shrugged, and then turned toward the jingling bell on the door of the shop. "Can I help you with anything else, Jed?"

"No, I'll just look around." Charlie, an old friend from school, didn't seem particularly interested in finches. Not everyone on the island knew about the dead finches at the crime scenes.

He wandered around the store for a few more minutes, poking his fingers into various cages containing rodents and reptiles. The store didn't carry cats or dogs, which spared him any feelings of guilt. Otherwise, he might've walked out of there with more pets than he could handle.

He'd had a dog at the time he was incarcerated, but Bowie had died when he was still locked up. Now he'd have to make do with Siggy.

"I know you!"

Jed's gaze bounced from the fish tank to a greasy-haired guy with big muscles and a paunch, pointing a finger at him. Jed's muscles coiled, and the corner of his eye twitched as he turned to face the man.

The guy dropped his arm and tried to suck in his gut. "You're Swain. Did time."

Jed continued to stare at the man, narrowing his eyes and setting his jaw. His hands curled into fists.

Shoving a hand through the lank strands of his hair, the man took a step back. "I—I'm not going off on you, man. I been there, done that with that bitch."

A light bulb popped on in Jed's head. This had to be Chase Thompson, Zoey's ex. He rolled his shoulders. "Nice way to refer to your ex-girlfriend who's just been murdered."

Chase snorted and swiped the back of his hand beneath his nose. "Didn't think you'd care, of all people."

"You'd be wrong."

"That b—girl stole money from me. Stole drugs, too. Looks like she finally crossed the wrong person."

The knots in Jed's gut tightened. "Yeah, well, if I were you, I wouldn't be talking ill of the dead. I heard the cops are still looking at you."

"I got an alibi." Chase's lip curled.

As Jed sauntered toward Chase, the other man's eyes widened, and he squared his shoulders. Jed brushed past him and said over his shoulder, "Everyone's got an alibi, dude."

Jed pushed out of the pet store and inhaled a deep breath of Dead Falls air, a mixture of seawater and pine. If that's the type of person Zoey had been hanging out with and stealing from, she'd been playing a dangerous game.

He glanced at his phone. Hannah hadn't contacted him yet, but she must be done with her sessions by now. He wanted a look inside Zoey's place for himself—maybe he might even find a clue there as to why she despised him enough to try to ruin his life.

He eyed Chase through the window, talking to Charlie, and then got into his truck. He texted Hannah, asking if she'd finished yet. She answered back immediately that she'd finished with her patients but had some notes to write up.

He'd waited eight years. He could wait a few more hours.

Chapter Ten

Hannah typed the last word and hit Save on Chrissy Boyd's file. The chatty little girl couldn't be more different from Sheldon, but her chatter had revealed nothing about her mother's killer.

She and her mom had shared burgers and fries from Gus's Grill in town for dinner, and then Chrissy had fallen asleep on the couch in front of the TV. She thought she heard her mother talking with someone, a man, but she also told Hannah about an elaborate dream with a unicorn flying over Dead Falls.

Kids' fertile imaginations and their inability to distinguish between reality and fiction made them difficult to treat in a therapeutic setting. A therapist had to be careful not to put words in a child's mouth.

Hannah snapped her laptop closed, eased off the couch and stretched her arms above her head. She dropped to the floor and gathered the dolls and furniture Chrissy had used to demonstrate what had happened on the last night of her mother's life.

As she cleaned up the rest of the toys, she cupped the little magnetic train she'd retrieved for Sheldon. He'd barely touched the toy he claimed he couldn't live without two nights ago, but Hannah had unraveled the reason why he wanted to return home—and it wasn't for the train cars.

He'd discussed a secret hiding place in his mom's trailer with her. The poor thing thought his mom might be hiding there. Hannah wasn't absolutely sure whether this hiding place existed or not, so she'd keep the police in the dark for now.

But that didn't mean she and Jed couldn't search for it tonight. Sheldon had mentioned his mother putting stuff in the wall. His imagination could be just as flighty as Chrissy's, but at least his account didn't include rainbow unicorns.

Jed had offered to pick her up tonight, so she wanted to get out of her schoolmarm outfit to make more of an impression. What kind of impression, she didn't have a handle on yet. His initial anger toward her had softened because it hadn't really been about anger. He'd wanted to push her away, pretend they didn't have a connection. Did he think his imprisonment would damage her in some way?

She'd known the charges against him had been a farce all along. What she hadn't discerned was that her father could've been behind the setup, but now she was determined to discover how that happened. She had to do it for the girl she'd been eight years ago.

She locked her office behind her and traipsed up to the main house, eyeing the new porch lights above her. What else could she do to make sure nobody trespassed on her property again to slink around? The person last night had to have been the killer. How else would he know about the dead birds? The police hadn't released that information—they didn't even know the birds held any significance until Jed told them.

Maybe there was some drug gang out there that used

finches for some reason. She snorted as she pushed through her front door. A drug cartel with a finch for a mascot didn't exactly inspire fear.

But the finch last night had terrified her.

An hour later, Hannah had showered and changed into a pair of light-colored jeans and a plain blue T-shirt. If they were going to be searching for secret compartments in Zoey's mobile home, she realized she should look ready for work—not like a prima donna. She shoved her feet into some canvas slip-ons to complete her dressed-down, unsexy look.

She set down Siggy's bowl with a fish dinner in it just as Jed's truck pulled up to the house. She sniffed her fingers and growled at Siggy. "You and your fish."

She opened the front door and waved at Jed, and then slipped back inside to wash her hands at the kitchen sink and squirt some lotion into her palm.

Patting the side pocket of her purse to make sure she had Zoey's keys, she strode out of the house and toward Jed's idling truck. She stepped onto the running board and slid into the passenger seat. "Hey."

Why did she suddenly feel like a teenager being picked up for a date?

"Hey, you." He maneuvered around her car in the circular drive, and the truck bounced as they headed for the road that ran in front of the property. "How'd the sessions go? And I don't mean any particulars."

"The sessions went as well as can be expected when dealing with two traumatized children." She hugged her purse to her chest. "But I do have one detail to share with you, and I don't think it's out of line for me to do so."

He raised his eyebrows. "If you say so."

"Remember the other night when Sheldon ran back to his home?"

"How could I forget it?" He flexed his fingers on the steering wheel. "He called me 'the bad man.'"

She waved her hand in the air to brush away the unpleasantness. "Do you remember why he made his way back there?"

"No." He lifted and dropped his shoulders quickly.

"He claimed it was because he left behind a favored toy, but I found out the real reason today."

"Yeah?" He paused while she sat there thinking about the ethics of revealing this information. "Are you gonna make me guess?"

She puffed out a breath. It was ethical if it helped nab Zoey's killer. "He said his mom had a secret compartment in the trailer."

"Maybe the police already located it and didn't find anything." He wagged his finger between the two of them. "Neither one of us knows what Seattle Homicide is investigating. We haven't seen their files. We don't know what avenues they're searching."

"I do. They're investigating the drug angle and that's it." She turned toward him, curling one leg beneath her. "I mean, that might be it, but they're not thinking outside the box at all. I would expect that from the Dead Falls Sheriff's Department, but you'd think Seattle PD would have more tools in their box."

"Every department wants a quick solve rate. That's why I got railroaded." He turned down the road leading to the mobile home park.

The homes were spaced far enough apart to yield no witnesses to Zoey's murder. Nobody had seen anyone unusual coming or going from her trailer, but they'd claimed noise from her neck of the park wasn't unusual.

Jed's lights blazed across the front of Zoey's trailer and the bedraggled yellow tape that had sunk to the ground. He pulled up to where he'd parked the previous time they'd driven to this spot.

Hannah dragged the key chain from her purse and said, "Let's get this show on the road. I'm going to leave my bag in your truck."

Their shoes crunched the gravel up to the door, and Hannah shook out the key and unlocked it. "There's a lamp here."

A soft yellow glow spilled over the living room, and everything was as she'd left it last time.

Jed pulled on a pair of gloves. "I don't need my prints to magically appear at this crime scene—or any other."

"I get it. You have a look around. I'm going to search for the secret hiding place."

He said, "In the wall."

"That's what Sheldon said." In the center of the room, she turned in a circle, eyeing the walls of the mobile home. They consisted of some kind of vinyl paneling. Zoey hadn't bothered decorating with any art or even school pictures.

A few large pieces of furniture hugged the walls—a brown velvet couch, its cushions still tossed, was on one side of the room facing a flat-screen TV. Next to the TV, a metal shelf that looked as if it belonged in a garage contained stacks of papers and napkins and ketchup packets from take-out joints around the island—including Gus's Grill. But Zoey and Sheldon had eaten pizza her last night instead of burgers.

A heavy, dark end table squatted next to the couch, the

shade on the lamp perched upon it askew. A bong sat on the other end table, brown residue clouding the glass. The cops hadn't even bothered to take it, but they wouldn't have left any drugs.

The mismatched bits of furniture didn't leave a lot of empty wall space, so Hannah started with the wall next to the kitchen. She swept a long-handled wooden spoon from the kitchen counter that separated the living room from the kitchen and began tapping the handle against the wall.

It gave off the deep bass sound of an empty space, which indicated a gap of some sort between the paneling and the wall of the trailer. She tapped the wall from just above her head down to her feet. She and Zoey had been about the same height, and she doubted Zoey would've chosen a hiding place she couldn't reach without a step stool.

She continued her search to the end table with the drug paraphernalia and knelt on the table to tap the wall above it. She skipped over the couch, which had a window above it, and bypassed the crooked lamp. She started again on the other side of the lamp. The noises she got in return didn't indicate anything different or unusual from any of the spaces.

As she crossed from the other side of the room, Jed emerged from the back of the home and asked, "Anything yet, Sherlock Holmes?"

"Nothing. You?" She turned toward him, clutching the spoon in her hand.

"What happened to her?" He swept his arm across the disheveled room. "Zoey did well in school, had normal parents—at least as normal as anyone else's—had hopes and dreams. How did it all end here in this mess?"

"She fell apart after the trial. Most people around here thought the rape changed her—as it would have if it had actually happened. She started using drugs, and it was all downhill from there." Hannah twirled the spoon in her fingers like a mini baton. "We stopped speaking after the trial. By the time I came back to the island, she had already had Sheldon and was on a downward slide."

Jed's jaw tightened into a hard line. "Maybe she turned to drugs to assuage her guilt—if she ever felt any. Sounds like she didn't if she were still pointing me out to her son as the bad guy."

"I can't tell you what was going on in her head." She waved the spoon in the air. "I'm going to check the other wall, though."

"I'll have a look in the kitchen." He swung open the first cupboard he got to and swore. "How did she feed her kid?"

Hannah turned her back on Jed's frustration and started tapping again. She'd covered a few feet toward the TV when the tenor of the noise changed. "Jed? I think I found something."

She struck the spoon against the panel on the left, the right and then the middle. "This middle panel sounds different—and it looks loose. It moved when I tapped it."

Jed came up behind her. "Which one?"

"This one." She pounded her fist against it, and the panel definitely moved.

"It's missing nails on the bottom portion." He dug his fingernails into the gaps between the panels and shifted the middle one to the side, revealing a dark crevasse. "Bingo."

Hannah dug her cell phone from her back pocket and turned on the flashlight. "How far does it go down?"

Peering inside the gap, Jed said, "There's a box in there, but you're going to have to retrieve it. My arm is too big to fit."

Jed scooted over and drew Hannah in front of him.

She'd been right about the height of the hiding place. It met her at eye-level. She stood on tiptoe and plunged her hand into the space. Her fingers brushed a cushioned lid and then crawled down the side to wedge beneath the bottom of the box.

She grasped the box and pulled it up, but it got stuck. "Zoey must've had more panels out when she placed the box in there because it won't fit through this hole."

Jed curled his fingers around the edge of the next panel, then yanked, and the panel cracked. He did the same thing to the other side, creating a gaping gash in the wall. "There you go."

She lifted the upholstered brown box from the hole. Gold-embossed curlicues decorated the sides. "Looks like a cigar box or something."

Holding the box in both hands as if it were a sacred offering, Hannah carried it to the sagging couch and sank onto the edge. With Jed hovering over her shoulder, she flipped up the lid with her thumbs.

Jed drew in a breath next to her. "That's a lot of cash. Maybe this *was* a drug deal gone bad."

Hannah could barely hear him over the roaring in her ears as she hooked a finger around the metal band of a watch and lifted it from the box, where it dangled and glittered in front of her eyes.

Jed whistled. "Expensive watch."

Hannah cranked her head to the side and blinked. "It was my father's."

Chapter Eleven

Hannah licked her dry lips. She didn't even have to examine the inscription on the back of the watch. She could pick it out from a pile of watches. Her mother had given her dad that watch when they first got engaged. It was the first possession of his that had signaled his ascension to the moneyed class. He'd bought other, more expensive watches since this one, but this marked a milestone in his social climbing.

Jed tossed a wad of bills back into the box. "What is Zoey doing with your dad's watch?"

Her gaze shifted to Jed's hands, curled into fists. "I know what you're thinking—that he gave her this watch as payment for setting you up—but I don't think so."

"I thought you were beginning to see things my way."

"Oh, I am." She twirled the watch around her finger as the links clinked together. "But my dad never would've given this up. It meant too much to him. Besides, why give her a watch when she'd prefer cash…and he had that, too."

"Maybe this." Jed poked his fingers at the rolled-up bills in the box.

"Maybe." She cupped the watch in her hand and squinted at the engraving on the back of the face—her parents' initials and the date of their engagement. "If he had given this watch to Zoey as a bribe, she would've hawked it by now. What good is this to her?"

Jed scratched his chin. "You think she stole it? When would she ever have had that opportunity?"

"When they were together planning your fall." She pinched the bridge of her nose. "I don't remember my dad wearing this watch after...after I left for college. But he didn't report it as stolen, either."

Jed took a few steps away from the couch. "The watch can't tell us much about Zoey's murder, but the cash can. Like I said before when you weren't listening, it could be drug money. She could've been playing fast and loose with her dealer's drugs and money, and he killed her for it. I ran into Chase in the pet store, and he even admitted Zoey was stealing from him."

"He must be confident in his alibi to be spreading around that bit of gossip."

"Yeah, I reminded him not to be so cocky. Alibis have a habit of disappearing in this town."

"It's just...odd." She thumbed through the money in the box, both stacks and rolls. "And what about Stephanie? Does she have a stash of money in her place, too? Two women who use drugs with no history of selling are murdered because they both decided, at the same time, to rip off their dealers?"

"When we give the money to the police, it's going to bolster that theory."

"But they can't make it stick to Stephanie."

Jed said, "They'll just assume the killer got the money back from her."

"Flimsy." She hung the heavy watch around her wrist.

"We'll tell them about the money, but they don't have to know about this watch."

"Why not? It's not as if your father could've had anything to do with Zoey's murder." Jed slid the secret panel back over the hole, which it no longer concealed due to the broken panels on either side.

She shook her arm, rattling the watch. "I'm conducting my own investigation, and I think this is a piece of that puzzle. What came first? Zoey's accusation against you? Or my father's suggestion to her that she trump up a charge?"

"I don't know, Hannah. Maybe you should just let it go. He's dead. I'm free. We're...friends again."

"Are we?"

He blew out his cheeks. "Let's get out of this dump. How are you going to explain Zoey's money to the cops?"

"I'm going to tell the truth. Sheldon mentioned a secret hiding place in the home, but I didn't tell them about it because I didn't know if it was a fantasy. I remembered I still had the keys from before, decided to take a look myself and discovered the money. They'll be grateful."

Jed snorted. "For being the daughter of a cop, you don't know cops very well."

"Now they can take their drug scenario and run with it."

"If that's the end of this." Jed dropped beside her on the couch and took the box from her lap. "And there's not another murder."

LESS THAN AN hour later, as the box sat on the floor under the seat and the watch was tucked away in Hannah's purse, Jed pulled his truck up to the curb a block from the best pizza place in town.

When he cut the engine, he sat in place, running his

hands along the steering wheel. "It'll probably be crowded in there. Luigi's always is."

"Yeah, so?" She already had her hand on the door handle.

"You sure you wanna be seen with me?" His lips twisted, but not into a smile.

She released the handle and grabbed his forearm. "Are you serious? Are you worried about the past or the present? You were exonerated almost three years ago, and you have strong alibis for both of these murders. Nobody is looking at you for this."

"I know, but…"

"You're an ex-con." She dug her fingernails into his arm. "Stop with the self-pity, Swain. Nobody cares."

Before he could answer, she released his arm and shoved open the door of the truck, hopping to the ground.

When he joined her on the sidewalk, she hooked her arm through his to show him she meant it. She wasn't ashamed of being seen with Jed Swain.

She kept a firm hold of him when they pushed through the door of the restaurant. The din of the room and the smell of garlic engulfed them. Nobody here seemed too concerned about the death of two local women.

A couple of guys from a rowdy corner table yelled out Jed's name and raised their beer mugs in his direction.

Jed's cheeks sported red flags at the attention, but he tipped two fingers in their direction to acknowledge their greeting. He mumbled in her ear, "All I need is a cheering section."

"It's better than torches and pitchforks." She walked up to the counter and tipped her head back to read the menu board. "Large deluxe? You need a salad?"

"No salad, but I'll take some of those garlic knots." He

dropped his gaze to the pimpled kid at the counter. "And a large soda."

The teen's finger hovered over the computer in front of him. "So, a large deluxe, order of garlic knots and something to drink for you, ma'am?"

Jed smirked beside her, and she elbowed him. "A glass of red wine, please."

Jed paid with a card and took his plastic cup to the soda machines while she scanned the room for a table.

Hannah made a beeline toward the waitress cleaning off a table for two, wedged next to a larger, round table occupied by a lively group of adults. She could live without the chattering people next to them, but at least they had a window view.

She scurried to the table, planted the plastic number on the clean surface and tossed her sweatshirt over the back of one chair. She smiled at the waitress. "Perfect timing."

"Yeah, it's crowded in here tonight." The waitress glanced over her shoulder at the front door. "They don't seem too bothered by those murders."

When she sniffed, Hannah did a double take at the young woman's red nose and smeared mascara. She put her hand on the waitress's arm. "Did you know the victims?"

Nodding, she plucked a napkin from the dispenser on the table. "Steph was a good friend of mine. She was a sweet person. She didn't deserve that."

"I'm sorry you lost your friend."

The waitress studied Hannah's face. "You're that therapist in town, aren't you?"

"I am." Hannah held her breath. Even if most people knew she was seeing Chrissy, she couldn't reveal that information.

"M-maybe I could talk to you sometime? I've never had a friend die before. I'm wrecked."

"Of course." Hannah slid a card from her purse and pressed it into the young woman's hand. "What's your name?"

"Shari Tremaine."

"Call me anytime, Shari."

Jed slowed his steps as he approached, his soda clutched in one hand and her wine in the other. He stepped aside for Shari and set the drinks on the table. "What was that about?"

"Never you mind." She pointed at her wine. "How'd you snag that? I thought they were bringing it to the table."

"I waylaid the guy carrying it over here. Thought you needed it sooner rather than later after your discovery tonight."

Jed pulled out her chair for her, and she collapsed in it. "It didn't stress me out so much as confuse me. I don't understand the connection between those two. My dad barely said hello to Zoey any of the times she was over at the house."

"He barely said hello to anyone. Doesn't mean he didn't notice them." He took the chair across from her. "He sure noticed me."

She took a sip of her wine, sweeter than she preferred, but not bad for the house wine at the local pizza joint. "Still haven't had a minute to search through that box…but I plan to do it."

"Knock yourself out. If you find anything in there about the current crimes, let me know." He stirred the ice in his Coke with his straw. "Damn, free refills and everything."

The noisy table behind Hannah began to break up, and someone touched her shoulder. She twisted her head around to find Bryan Lamar, the elementary school principal, turned around in his chair.

"Dr. Maddox, can I have a word?"

"Call me Hannah." She'd met with Mr. Lamar a few times regarding students that the school nurse had referred to her.

"And you can call me Bryan." He tipped his head toward his table companions now saying goodbye to each other and figuring out a tip. "Just a little casual get-together with the staff before school starts, but we were talking about our two students."

He didn't have to tell her which two students. Sheldon would be starting third grade if he stayed on the island, and Chrissy would be in second. "You know I can't…"

He held up one hand. "Of course, but if there's anything the teachers can do, if and when the kids come into the classroom, we'd appreciate a heads-up."

"Got it, Bryan. Probably just clamp down on the gossip for now." Her gaze flicked to two female teachers who had stopped haggling over money and seemed to have their heads bent this way.

"Absolutely. We can do that. We'll do our best for the kids, but I'd like to meet with you before they return to the classroom."

"Sounds like a good idea." She scrambled through her purse, looking for business cards and gave up. She handed him her phone, instead. "Fresh out of business cards. Call yourself from my cell, and I'll add you to my contacts. You do the same, and we'll touch base."

Bryan tapped her phone and handed it back to her. "Looking forward to it."

His coworkers called to him at the door, and he gave

Hannah a shrug as he followed their path through the crowded restaurant.

Jed hunched forward. "Who's that guy?"

"Principal of Samish Elementary."

"Good old Samish." He slurped at his drink. "Told you everyone and his cousin knows about you and the kids."

"Well, he *is* the principal, but it's not a stretch to imagine that a lot of people know I'm working with them." She ran a thumb over the lipstick imprint on her wineglass.

"Not sure about that, but the current department doesn't seem any more competent than previous departments on this island. Loose lips and all that. Charlie at the pet store didn't seem to have a clue about the birds."

"What did she have to say on the matter?" Hannah sealed her lips and moved her wineglass as Shari returned to their table bearing their pizza and knots. She eked out a small smile at Hannah as she placed the pizza on the metal stand in the middle of the table and dropped the basket of knots beside it. "Can I get you anything else?"

Jed picked up a greasy knot between his fingers and inhaled. "This is all I need."

Hannah rolled her eyes. "We're good, Shari." Shari backed away from the table and practically fled back to the kitchen, even though a group of people hovering at the empty teachers' table called after her.

"What's her deal?" Jed sank his teeth into the little ball of dough in his hand.

Hannah put her finger to her lips. "Friends with Stephanie Boyd."

Jed stopped chewing as his gaze sought out the rattled waitress. "Hit her hard, huh?"

"You could say that." Hannah jiggled a piece of pizza loose from the whole pie and plopped it onto her plate.

"If she's friends with Stephanie, maybe I should talk to her."

"Don't." She fanned her hand over the slice on her plate. "She'll think I told you."

"I *am* working for Stephanie's brother, and he gave me a list of her friends on the island. Even though Shari's name wasn't on that list, I just added it."

"Just keep me out of it. I don't want her to think I'm the kind of therapist who blabs about my business." She pulled at a string of cheese hanging from her pizza and popped it in her mouth before taking a bite.

"I won't say a word about you. She probably wouldn't recognize me, anyway."

"Right." She dabbed a napkin at her lips.

"What's that supposed to mean? You think everyone in town knows my sad story?"

"Are you seriously fishing for compliments right now?" She took a big gulp of wine, the warmth of it in her belly making her bold. "Any woman who doesn't remember you needs her head examined by doctors more powerful than I."

She chased her gulp of wine with another, and then snuck a peek at Jed's face.

Fiddling with his straw, he gazed over her shoulder at the wall. "How come you don't have a serious boyfriend?"

"That's a dodge…or another set up for a compliment." She attacked her pizza.

"That's where your father screwed up." He stuffed another knot in his mouth and dusted his fingers over his napkin. "He should've never destroyed your letters to me. We would've corresponded for a while, and you would've grown bored with the whole thing. Instead, you romanticized the situation and me."

"Shut up." She crumpled up her napkin and threw it at him. "Don't try to analyze the analyst. Believe me, I do not hold a romanticized vision of you. Just look at the way you're shoveling those disgusting garlic knots into your face."

He chuckled, further breaking the tension between them. "Doesn't compare to the way you keep pulling cheese off your pizza and sucking it off your fingers."

"I am not sucking cheese from my fingers. That's obviously your fantasy."

They laugh-snorted for several seconds until a man approached their table, his gnarled hands gripped in front of him, the smile on his ancient, brown face uncertain. "Jed Swain?"

Jed grabbed a napkin and wiped his eyes. When he got a closer look at the man, his eyes widened. "Roaming Bear?"

The man cracked a smile, displaying a missing canine. He thumped a fist against his concave chest. "Not roaming so much anymore. I heard about your exoneration three years ago and knew you'd moved back to the island. Meant to drop by, but my wife had a stroke a few years back and well, like I said, I don't roam no more. But she does like her Luigi's pizza."

"Sorry to hear about your wife." Jed gestured toward Hannah. "You know Hannah Maddox, right?"

Roaming Bear's dark eyes pierced Hannah as he nodded once. "Was glad to hear you got justice at last, even though most of us knew you were innocent from the get-go."

"I appreciate your belief in me. Hannah always believed in me, too."

Hannah folded her hands in her lap. Jed didn't have to defend her against a member of the Samish nation. She knew they'd hated her father—for good reason.

She cleared her throat and grabbed a chair from the table next door. "Do you want to have a seat while you wait for your pizza?"

Roaming Bear studied her face for several seconds. "Sure."

Jed jumped up to pull the chair up to their table and help the old man settle into it. Then he shoved the basket of knots toward him. "Help yourself."

Roaming Bear's eyes never left Hannah's face as he said, "No, thanks. Garlic doesn't agree with me these days."

As Jed opened his mouth to say more, Roaming Bear cut him off. "You're seeing those two kids whose mothers were murdered, aren't you?"

Ugh, Hannah didn't want to give the old man even more reason to dislike her, but she shook her head. "I can't discuss whether or not I'm treating anyone."

"Yeah, yeah, I understand." He poked a bent finger at her. "That's a good thing you do, helping kids."

Hannah eased out a tiny breath. At least he didn't completely hate her.

Jed grinned like a proud parent. As he pulled off a piece of pizza, he said, "Roaming Bear, you've been around forever and seem to know everything there is to know about Dead Falls. What do you know about the significance of finches? Any Samish folklore surrounding them?"

"Finches." Roaming Bear put his finger on the side of his prominent nose. "No legends surrounding finches. Just a bird, as far as I know."

"And you would know," Jed replied.

"But I do remember that family who collected them here on the island."

Jed dropped his pizza. "Some family collected finches? Who?"

"You wouldn't know them. This was about thirty years ago, out Misty Hollow way. Probably a few years before the two of you were even born. I don't even think your father was sheriff at that time."

"Not thirty years ago." Hannah curled her fingers around the stem of her wineglass.

"Who were they and why did they collect finches?" Jed planted his elbow on the table and his palm cupped his jaw.

"The Keldorfs."

"Now that name sounds familiar. Some tragedy there." Hannah raised her glass to her lips, the wine's pungent aroma suddenly making her head throb.

"Oh, I'd say it was a tragedy, all right. Chet Keldorf murdered his whole family and then killed himself. Only two of the foster kids survived, and after he killed his family and before he turned the shotgun on himself...he killed all the finches."

Chapter Twelve

Dead finches. Jed shot a quick look at Hannah's rounded eyes and gave a slight shake of his head. "Where did this happen? Where did the Keldorfs live?"

"Um." Roaming Bear raised his dark eyes to the ceiling, as if looking for the answer up there. He found it. "On the other side of the falls—not too far from your old place, which I heard you're fixing up."

"W-were the two foster kids injured?" Hannah had such a tight grip on her wineglass, she looked close to snapping the stem.

"Don't think so. Law enforcement whisked them right out of there." Roaming Bear's eyes softened as he looked at Hannah. "You really care about children, don't you? Unfortunately, two other children did die in the melee. Two other foster kids. As I recall, the Keldorfs couldn't have kids of their own and fostered several over the years."

"CPS obviously didn't do a great job of vetting Mr. Keldorf." Hannah hunched her shoulders and finished off the dregs of her wine, looking like she needed more.

Roaming Bear held up one unsteady finger. "I think I just heard my number. I need to get this pizza home to my Rose."

"I'll grab it." Jed pushed back his chair and strode toward

the counter. By the time he returned to the table carrying the box, Hannah was standing next to Roaming Bear's chair, helping him to his feet.

The old man patted her hand and whispered something in her ear, which made her smile.

Jed held out the pizza to Roaming Bear. "Do you need help with this out to your car?"

"No, no. Finish your meal. Rose will be pleased to hear I saw you out tonight. Nice to meet you, Hannah. Take care, boy." He shuffled out of the restaurant, holding the pizza in front of him as someone held the door open.

Jed picked up his slice. "What did he say to you?"

"Told me I was nothing like my old man, which I take as a compliment."

"Especially from Roaming Bear." He took a big bite and chewed, waiting for Hannah to bring up the Keldorfs. By the time he swallowed, she was still staring into her empty glass.

He dragged a napkin across his face. "So, what do you think about the Keldorfs?"

"Just thinking about family annihilators and how we can see the signs."

Roaming Bear's story had engaged her psychology mind, but Jed needed her investigative mind. "But the finches. Don't you think that's a coincidence? Dead finches then, dead finches now."

"That is strange, but Chet Keldorf is dead. He's not killing women today and leaving dead birds."

"Yeah, but it's the first clue we've gotten about these finches. Maybe that crime inspired someone else. Maybe Keldorf has a relative still living in the area. Doesn't psychopathy run in families?"

"There is a genetic component, usually passed down from the father."

Jed hit the table. "There you go."

"Didn't you hear Roaming Bear? Chet Keldorf didn't have any children. He didn't pass his genes down to anyone."

"Siblings, nephews, then." He waved his crust at her. "I want to pursue this lead."

"It's the only one we have." She pushed her plate away with a half-eaten piece of pizza on it. "Are we going to the police with this one?"

He answered, "Do you think they'd spend any time looking into it?"

"No. We'll do it ourselves. They may already have the Keldorf crime on their radar. They have a lot more resources and access to a lot more databases than we do." She crumpled up her napkin. "Are you done?"

"Are you kidding?" He lifted the basket with two garlic knots rolling in the bottom. "I have two of these bad boys left."

"Put them in the to-go box I'm going to get for the rest of this pizza."

"Do you want another glass of wine? I'm driving."

"Actually, the wine made me tired. I'm ready to call it a night." She rose from her seat and said over her shoulder, "I'll get that to-go box."

Jed kept his eyes on Hannah's stiff back as she walked to the counter. She didn't seem tired at all. She practically vibrated with energy.

He'd demolished one of the knots and was eyeing the second one before Hannah got back with the box.

As she loaded the leftover pizza into the box with quick

movements, Jed circled her wrist with his fingers. "You wanna tell me what's up? You've been distracted and jumpy at the same time ever since we heard Roaming Bear's story about the Keldorfs."

She adjusted the pizza in the box and secured the lid on the box. "It's the name—Keldorf."

"Yeah, you mentioned you'd heard it before. I have to confess the crime sounded familiar, but I don't think I ever got the name because no Keldorfs remained on the island."

"The name's not on the island anymore—except in my attic."

Jed tugged on his earlobe. "You mean among your old man's things?"

"Exactly. When I was up there looking for info on your arrest, I saw the Keldorf name on a box—a very old-looking box."

"I thought your father wasn't the sheriff thirty years ago."

"He wasn't the sheriff, but he was a deputy. I'm sure that type of crime on the island would require the entire force to work it. My father must've been involved. He either kept notes at the time, or he took material from the station when he retired."

"Why would he be interested in the Keldorf crime? Murder-suicide seems pretty straightforward to me."

"I don't know. I'm beginning to think I didn't know my father at all." She patted the pizza box. "But if we're going to look into the Keldorfs and their dead finches, we have a place to start."

"Now? You mean start now?" He cocked his head. "I thought the wine had made you tired."

"I was just trying to get rid of you." She brushed her hands together and hitched her purse over her shoulder.

Slapping a hand against his chest, he said, "Me? I thought we were in this together. Why would you cut me out?"

She drew her bottom lip between her teeth. "I wasn't sure you'd want to have a look in those boxes. You seemed uninterested in the one for your own case."

"Really? That was *my* case." He sucked down the rest of his soda and slammed it on the table. "I'm all in for looking into someone else's sorry life."

JED BLEW OUT a breath as he pulled behind Hannah's car and saw the porch lights still glowing brightly. "At least nobody has defaced your property tonight."

Hannah screwed up her mouth on one side. "Not that we know of. This is a big property."

"That's what concerns me—you out here all alone at night." He cut the engine and the silence around them confirmed his fears. "You ever learn how to shoot one of your daddy's pistols?"

"I did, and I still have them…in storage."

"Not doing much good there, are they?" He opened the door of his truck, and the sole of his shoe crunched the gravel. He made a beeline for the front door to check for dead birds and broken glass.

The curtain at the front window flicked and he stumbled back.

Hannah came up behind him and patted him on the shoulder. "That's just Siggy the watch cat."

"Too bad he didn't scare off the intruder last night." Jed snapped his fingers. "How about a dog?"

Shoving her key in the lock, Hannah clicked her tongue. "Siggy doesn't like dogs."

Jed's muscles coiled as Hannah stepped into the foyer.

The fixture burned brightly, high in the ceiling above them, casting a warm glow over the entryway. He swept past her, taking the two steps down to the family room, its large windows facing to the forest on the side of the house.

Leaving the lights off in the family room, he crept toward the plates of glass, feeling exposed, and peered at the dark trees huddled beyond the property line. He leaned his forehead against the cool glass. "Anybody could be out here staring inside. Where are those guns?"

"We're in luck." She jerked both thumbs at the ceiling. "The guns are in the same place as my father's case files— the attic."

"You get the Keldorf box, and I'll grab those guns...or at least the one I think is most appropriate for you."

"Most appropriate?" She wedged her hands on her curvy hips. "The pink one?"

He gave her a little shove. "The one you'll be able to use to take out an intruder. I can't imagine Mad Dog Maddox with a pink weapon."

She crooked her finger at him. "Follow me. It's one of those pull-down doors from the ceiling."

"My favorite kind." He traipsed up the staircase behind her.

She stopped beneath a square door and waved at the rope hanging down. "You probably don't even need a step stool to grab it, do you?"

"Let's see." He sidled next to her, stood on his tiptoes and grabbed the rope. He gave it a yank, and the trapdoor opened, ejecting a set of accordion steps. "Is there a light up there?"

"I think there used to be, but it must be broken." She

opened the drawer of a side table in the hallway and pulled out a flashlight. "This isn't my first trip up here, obviously."

"Then, after you." He made a flourish with his arm. Following her up also gave him the opportunity to appreciate her assets.

Hannah grabbed the sides of the ladder and started to ascend. She stopped suddenly about halfway up. "And stop eyeing my backside."

"Don't flatter yourself, Maddox."

When she reached the gaping space, she leaned forward to climb into the attic.

His palms itched to give her an assist by placing them on the aforementioned backside, but she'd probably smack him. "You good?"

"Yeah." She poked her head out, her hair hanging on either side of her face. "It's a little dusty."

"I've been in prison. What's a little dust?"

She pulled back, probably not knowing whether to laugh or cry. With his arms level with the opening, he hoisted himself into the attic, Hannah's bobbing flashlight creating a kaleidoscope of images.

Jed sniffed. "Was this his own private space, or what?"

"Mom made him move his stuff up here when it started cluttering the office, but I've never seen some of this stuff." She hunched over and made her way to a stack of boxes that looked as if she'd disturbed it before.

"Where are the guns?" He pulled his phone from his pocket and turned on the flashlight.

"In the corner, near the snowboards."

He also had to bend forward to move through the space. Crouching down in front of the snowboards, he ran his hand through the dusty lid of a gun safe. "These are locked up. Do you have the combination?"

"Zero, four, two, six."

He looked up. "Significance?"

"My parents' wedding anniversary—April 26. Basically, the day my father became a member of the moneyed class."

Jed ran a thumb along the combo lock and entered the code. It clicked open, echoing in the space. Five guns gleamed against the plush red interior of the case. He feathered his fingertips across the Glock 17. "Hello, beautiful."

"You talking to me or the gun?" Hannah puffed a lock of hair from her face.

He plucked the gun from its place and caressed it in his hands. "This little charmer."

"You want me to leave you two alone up here?"

"This one's perfect for you, Hannah. Do you know your gun safety, or should we go through that before I clean it up and load it?"

"We're talking about my father here. Of course, he taught me gun safety, although he never actually gave me a gun of my own."

"Maybe this was your mother's. It's definitely a piece for a feminine hold."

"My mom?" She snorted and then sneezed. "No way."

He closed the lid on the gun safe and scrambled the combination. "Did you find the Keldorf box?"

She rapped her knuckles on the lid of a cardboard box. "Right here. You wanna trade? That gun looks a lot lighter than this box."

"Sure." He checked the gun's chamber. "Unloaded. I'll buy you some ammo."

He handed her the gun and bent down to test the heft of

the box. As he couldn't stretch to his full height in the attic, he elected to shove the box toward the opening with his feet. Peering over the edge, he said, "How'd you get that other box down from here?"

"Very carefully. Why don't you get settled on the ladder, and then I'll hand the box to you?"

He maneuvered down the steps and then dropped the box on the floor, amid a flurry of dust. Then he turned to help Hannah down the rest of the way, as she clutched the Glock in one hand.

She hopped off the last step and fell against his chest. His arms went around her as naturally as breathing.

He inhaled her scent, musty attic and all, before he released her.

She skirted around him. "I'll clear a space on the coffee table. Let's dig through this."

He picked up the box and followed her to the family room. Her nervous hands fluttered around the table, moving items out of the way. He settled the box in the center and flipped off the lid.

Hannah sat on the floor, crossing her legs. "This stuff is old. I wonder why he kept it."

"Maybe because it was the biggest case of his career on the island. We haven't had too many murders here, and this one was horrific." He tapped the side of the box.

They leafed through the box, skimming her father's notes. "Doesn't make much sense." As she reached the bottom, she fanned out papers on the table and smoothed a map with her hand.

Jed leaned over her shoulder. "What's that?"

"It's a map of the Keldorf property." She tapped the paper with her index finger. "I do know this house. It's beyond the falls in Misty Hollow. Nobody has lived there for years. I just thought it had been someone's second home that they let go to rot. Now it makes sense. Who'd want to live where a crime like that occurred?"

"The owner could always raze it and rebuild—kinda like I'm doing with my family home." He traced his finger along the map, judging the distance to his place.

"What happened in your home doesn't compare with this." She flicked her finger at the paper in his hands. Rising to her knees, she snatched the map from him. "I have an idea."

He eyed her over the top of the paper. "What?"

"Let's check out this property. You know it's not something the sheriff's department or PD is going to do, but it's something we can investigate."

"What are we going to investigate?" Jed spread his hands. Maybe he never should've gotten Hannah involved in this case. She had her part to play, and he had his.

"I'm not sure, but my father thought something was amiss. He wouldn't have saved this information. He wouldn't have tagged and questioned aspects of it. And now we have dead finches at two murder scenes that mimic the dead birds at this one. I think it's worth digging into." She clambered to her feet, clutching the map in her hand.

Jed's mouth dropped open. "Now? You don't waste any time, do you?"

"Better to do it at night, undercover. We don't want to signal to anyone that we're looking at this thirty-year-old murder."

"You mean signal the killer because I'm pretty sure Seattle PD couldn't care less if we were sniffing around this property."

"Maybe that is what I mean." She waved the paper in the air. "Are you in, or what? Because I'm heading over there, with or without you."

"I've created a monster." He smacked his forehead with his palm, but he stood up and asked for a flashlight.

Jed didn't need a map or GPS to find the old Keldorf place in Misty Hollow. His truck crawled across the bridge to the other side of the island, slowing down to take in the falls to their right. The island had been named for the falls, which fell dead straight from the swirling water above them. The adventurous could walk behind the falls on a narrow path, taking a peek from the other side, but the water would be close enough to touch. The linear drop of the falls with no arc didn't allow a lot of space behind it and gave the falls its name.

The area had seen its fair share of deaths, both accidents and suicides. People did stupid stuff around nature, and hidden caves on either side of the falls attracted teens—attracted him and Hannah.

"Still takes my breath away." Hannah touched the glass as a fine mist clouded the passenger window. "Looks even more magnificent at night."

"With some moonlight." He sped up and crossed the bridge, not willing to go down memory lane with Hannah right now.

When they'd first discovered their friendship and easy camaraderie had blossomed into something more exciting, they'd spend many nights on the shore of the river—her side of the river—gazing out at the falls and making childish promises to each other. Then they'd ventured to the caves next to the falls for a few make-out sessions. If he'd never fallen for Hannah like that, her old man never would've come after him—but he still didn't spend one second regretting it.

His truck bounced as it exited the bridge, and he made a sharp right. "Nobody comes this way anymore. There aren't many properties in Misty Hollow, so it's not like people are driving past the Keldorf place on a daily basis as a reminder of what happened there."

"It's the kind of thing most small towns want to put behind them, isn't it? Murder-suicide involving children. Lots of missed red flags for a lot of people and agencies."

"Honestly, until Roaming Bear mentioned it tonight, I'd never even heard any of the Samish elders talk about it."

"Out of sight, out of mind—for most people. The dead finches are too much of a coincidence for me to buy."

"I don't know what you expect to find out here."

"I just see it as an opportunity to look at the place of the original dead finches before law enforcement descends and takes away our access to any evidence."

He aimed the truck down a narrow access road. "You really believe LE is going to descend on this place?"

"If they can't find the drug connection between the two crimes, they may very well look at other motives and scenarios, which may lead them right here." She pulled her sweatshirt around her body. "I just want to get a jump on them. I'm sure their investigation will lead them here eventually, even though they didn't seem very excited about the dead bird on my porch."

"That definitely could've been a prank, Hannah. Why would the killer target you?" He slowed the truck as a dilapidated house came into view, lit up by his headlights.

A structure that looked like a barn squatted to the right of the house, and a chicken coop had fallen over on its side.

"Well, this is creepy." Hannah had the door of the truck open before it came to a full stop and had one leg dangling out before he cut the engine. "The constant mist from the falls doesn't help."

Jed left the lights on and transferred his gun from inside the center console to the pocket of his denim jacket. He didn't like the looks of this place, even without its history of murder and mayhem.

He jumped from the truck and flicked on the flashlight Hannah had given him. She had her own aggressively thrust in front of her, as she stalked toward the house.

He grabbed the hood on her sweatshirt, and she stumbled backward. "Sorry. Where are you going in such a hurry?"

Tugging at her sweatshirt, she straightened it out. "I want to see where the finches were killed. The report said he reached into the cages and twisted their little necks and then left them where they dropped, so that there were a few cages containing dead birds. Why'd he do that? Why kill your pets?"

Jed said, "I've read about people who killed their dogs and cats before killing themselves. You're the psychologist. Doesn't it have something to do with not wanting to take that journey by yourself?"

"That's one reason, but birds? You wanna take that journey with a bunch of birds?" She twisted a lock of hair around her finger. "Or maybe, like my dad's notes indicated, someone else killed the birds. Chet Keldorf didn't have any scratches on his hands. If you reached into a cage and started strangling birds, wouldn't they peck at you or claw your hand with their feet trying to get away?"

"You're asking me?" He thumped a hand on his chest. "I'm no bird expert."

"But you are a PI." She tugged on his sleeve. "Let's go inside."

They approached the house, its dark windows staring out at them, daring them to come inside. The door had an open slash down the front where the wood had rotted away from the constant moisture in the air, and it tilted to one side, favoring its good hinge.

He tapped the door with the toe of his shoe, and it gaped away from the frame. "At least we don't have to bust in." Holding it open, he said, "In this case, I'm going to break the code of chivalry and enter before you. Keep your flashlight trained in front of me."

Jed turned sideways and squeezed his body through the opening. He swept his flashlight across the room, still furnished.

Hannah put one leg through the gap in the door and nudged him. "Move it."

He took a few more steps into the room, the wood floor creaking beneath his feet. "Must've been a pretty nice place at one point."

"I don't think CPS would've allowed those foster kids in here if it weren't. At least they got that part right. Should've been looking more closely at Mr. Keldorf."

"How come we never came here as teenagers? Seems to me this would've been the perfect spot to party and make out." He quirked his eyebrows up and down.

"We had our own places for that." She tiptoed through the room as if fearful of waking the dead. Parking in front of a table pushed against the wall, she said, "This is it. The cages are still here."

He came up behind her, flicking his light across the metal cages stationed on the table, the bars glinting in the darkness. "Roaming Bear seems to think Keldorf killed the birds after he murdered his family. I should've asked him how he knew that."

"Probably a solid guess. The foster kids were old enough to realize something would be off if he killed all his birds. From all accounts, he surprised them. All the bodies were in different locations, so while they may have heard the gunshots, they wouldn't have known the targets. Blasts from rifles aren't all that uncommon, as you know."

"And the other kids survived, how?"

"They hid in a hollowed-out log in the forest. They didn't come out until a deputy arrived on a call about the Keldorf's cow wandering in the road."

"These were the older foster kids, right? So maybe they heard the gunshots and took cover. They were old enough to have figured out their foster dad wasn't right in the head and put two and two together when they heard the rifle shots."

"Ugh, so horrible for everyone." Hannah took a turn around the room, her flashlight bobbing in front of her. "The murders of Zoey and Stephanie certainly aren't re-enactments of this crime, except for the presence of children. Their kids are about the same age as the dead foster children were."

"So…motive?"

She chewed on her bottom lip. "Family of the murdered foster kids taking revenge on Dead Falls for not doing enough to protect them?"

"Seems like a stretch. Why pick on single moms?" He held up a hand as she opened her mouth. "But definitely worth looking into the identity of those children. You can use your connections with Maggie to dig further."

They spent the next several minutes shuffling through the abandoned home, the beams from their flashlights criss-crossing each other. Jed didn't know what else Hannah was looking for, but she seemed satisfied as she took one last look at the empty birdcages.

"I guess that's it. Doesn't look like anyone has been here for years." Hannah jerked a thumb over her shoulder. "Do you want to take a quick peek in the barn? I didn't realize the Keldorf place was a farm."

"After you this time." Jed pushed the broken door away from the frame for Hannah to slip through. When he clambered through, more wood cracked away from the frame. "Oops."

By the time he'd put the pieces back in place, Hannah was halfway across the yard on her way to the barn. Swearing, he jogged after her. The snap of a stick from the woods beyond slowed his gait as he swung his flashlight in the direction of the noise and held his breath.

Night birds rustled in the trees, and Jed blew out the breath, following Hannah into the barn. This door still swung easily on its hinges, and he pulled it closed behind them.

Hannah, on her tiptoes and peering into a stall, called over her shoulder. "Looks like someone may have been sleeping here recently. The hay is fresh, and there's a blanket."

He sidled up next to her, draping an arm over her shoulders. "Homeless? Maybe some randy teenagers who don't mind the creep factor."

"The hinges on the door seemed oiled, too. I doubt teens

would be that responsible." She dropped down to her heels and ducked beneath his arm.

She went one direction in the small barn, and he went the other way. He said, "I don't remember anything about the barn in that file, do you? I don't think any of the victims were discovered here."

"They were all in the house."

Jed scuffed up to a small pen in the corner, about waist-high, covered with chicken wire. "What the hell is this?"

Hannah appeared next to him and crouched down to push at the door. "For chickens? A pig?"

Jed scanned the contents of the pen with his flashlight, zeroing in on grooves in the wood on the side. "Chicken scratches?"

"What?" Hannah had opened the door and crawled partially inside.

"To your left. Do you see the carvings in the wood?"

Hannah inched forward on her hands and knees and gasped. "They're words that say, *help me, save me.*"

Jed spun around as the barn door clacked. Seconds later, a glass smashed against the walls, exploding in a fiery crash.

Chapter Thirteen

Hannah screamed and backed out of the pen. The heat from the fire already warming her face.

Jed grabbed her arm and half dragged her to the barn door. He shoved his body against it, but it wouldn't budge. He shouted, "Hey! Someone locked us inside."

Despite the heat, Hannah felt an icy chill slide down her spine. She threw herself against the solid door, bruising her shoulder for her efforts.

"We're not getting out through the door." With his body, Jed blocked her from the fire raging in the stall, contained for now, and propelled her in the other direction toward the small window.

He whipped out his gun and shot through the glass a few times until it cracked in several places. He took the butt of his gun and struck the window repeatedly until he punched out the window. The flames leaped behind them, grateful for the air.

Jed hoisted her up. "Crawl through."

Bicycling her legs, Hannah said, "You're not going to fit through there."

"I'll find another way out." He practically tossed her through the window, and she landed on the ground.

The fire lit up the area around the barn, and she noticed rusty tools in a wheelbarrow. She staggered to the wheelbarrow and grabbed the handle of an axe.

She dragged the axe on the ground behind her as she stumbled back to the blazing barn. She yelled at the window. "Jed, I have an axe. I can hand it to you through the window."

"Go, go!"

She nearly folded from the relief of hearing his voice, loud and strong. She heaved the axe above her head and fed it through the window.

"Stand back, Hannah."

She retreated to the wheelbarrow as the barn emitted sounds of thumps and splintering wood, along with the cracks and pops of the fire. Pieces of the wall began to fly out as Jed battered his way through the structure with the axe.

As she watched, her hands covering her mouth, Jed crashed through the barn wall, coughing and sputtering.

She rushed toward him, her hands scrambling for his jacket, pulling him away from the inferno. Several yards away from the fire, they collapsed in the cool mulch of the forest floor.

Jed hoisted himself against a tree and fumbled in his pocket for his gun. "Someone out here threw a Molotov cocktail into that barn and locked us in. He could still be lurking around."

Hannah picked up the axe he'd dropped at his feet and held it across her body. "Let him try."

Squeezing her hand, he said, "I appreciate the help, but you'd be better off calling 911."

She placed the axe across her thighs and retrieved her phone. "You need the paramedics, too. You look…singed."

"I'm fine." He snatched her phone from her hand. "We need to call 911. The sirens might scare him away. Oh, pass code."

She rattled off four digits, and Jed's finger hovered over the numbers. "That's the date and month of my release."

Her cheeks blazed hotter than that fire as she grabbed the phone. "I know."

She jerked her head to the side as a twig snapped, and she tapped in 911 with a shaky finger. When she finished the call, she turned to Jed. "Why would someone want to destroy that barn with us in it? These current murders have to be connected to the Keldorf crimes. Someone followed us here, or they were watching. Maybe they're sleeping here. We saw evidence of a recent inhabitant. And what was that pen for? Was someone imprisoned there?"

"You're making my head swim—or it's the smoke I inhaled." He rubbed his eyes with sooty knuckles. "Maybe we turn this all over to Seattle Homicide and let them do their jobs. Back away."

She hacked up a lung and swiped a hand under her nose. "You're directing that at me, aren't you? How can *you* back away? You promised Michael to investigate his sister's murder. You want *me* to back away."

"Is that such a bad idea?" He trailed his fingers along the palms she'd scraped hauling tail out of that window. "You have a job to do. Look after those kids. Even if they know nothing about the murder of their mothers, they're going to need help navigating this trauma. You can do that."

Digging the heels of her running shoes into the forest floor, she said, "I can do more than that."

"It's not just the kids, is it? You feel guilty about Zoey because you two used to be friends, and her life went off the rails. That's not your fault, Hannah. She made those choices in life." His jaw clenched into a hard line. "Bad ones."

"I know it's not my fault, but she was my friend once, and there's something about Sheldon that hits me right here." She pounded a fist against her chest. "I mean, Chrissy, too, of course."

The wail of the sirens in the distance cut off any further argument from Jed. She didn't mention to him that she planned to read her father's notes on the Keldorf case more thoroughly. Her father may not have been the most ethical sheriff, but he'd had damned good cop instincts. And she'd inherited them.

As HANNAH TOOK a swig of water from the bottle the paramedics handed to her, Jed pulled away from the firebombed barn and the firefighters still sifting through and extinguishing the debris. They had both refused treatment, although Jed received some salve for the burns on the back of his neck and hands.

The truck bounced over the dirt road, and Jed flexed his fingers on the steering wheel. "We could always go back to see if any part of that pen remains."

"I don't understand why the deputies on the scene wouldn't notify the Seattle contingent after what we told them." Hannah smoothed a spot of soot on her jeans with her thumb.

"Maybe because we sounded completely demented, talking about a thirty-year-old murder-suicide, dead finches and words carved into the side of a pig pen." Bracing his hands on the wheel, he lifted his shoulders. "We can always check in with Detective Howard Chu tomorrow and tell him what we discovered."

"That was not a pig pen, and we don't even know if any of it survived the fire." She clasped her hands between her bouncing knees. "Do you think that's why our stalker threw the firebomb? He wanted to destroy the evidence in the barn?"

"What evidence? We have no idea who carved those words in the wood and why. What significance does it possibly have for the current murders? We know the women weren't held there, or anywhere."

She turned in her seat, pulling her seat belt away from her sore shoulder. "It has to mean something, Jed. Were we followed, or was someone already watching that barn or sleeping there? Why not let us look around and return when we left? Why try to destroy the barn? Why try to…kill us?"

She expected pushback from Jed, braced for it, even. Instead, he coughed and shook his head. "I don't know."

His quiet words amped up the fear already stirring in her belly, and she folded her arms across her midsection. "We gotta speak to the Seattle detectives tomorrow. I still need to return the keys to Zoey's trailer. Nobody has even asked me for them. What exactly are they investigating?"

"They must be going all in on the drug angle. I'm sure they're still looking at Chase. He knew both women, dated one, sold them product. Makes sense."

She sighed. "If they had anything on Chase, he'd be behind bars by now. His alibi must be solid, or they have absolutely no evidence linking him to the murders."

"Maybe we should track down Keldorf's brother, Nate."

"Let's do it. He might be more willing to talk to us than the police."

"I doubt the cops are going to be interested in talking to Nate Keldorf." He pulled into her driveway. "Are you going to be okay tonight?"

She'd probably be okay, but she didn't want Jed to leave, not without knowing who threw that Molotov cocktail into the barn. She'd noticed Jed watching the rearview on the way here, but Dead Falls was a small town. Everyone knew she lived in the biggest house on the island—alone.

"D-do you want to come in?" She waved her hands. "I mean, you could clean up a bit more here. I could make us some tea with honey for our throats."

She cracked open the door of the truck, as if it meant no difference to her whether or not he came inside.

"Of course, yeah." He cut the engine. "I'm not comfortable leaving you alone out here, at least not until I get you some ammo for that gun."

She scooted out of the truck before he could change his mind, but he still beat her to the porch, scanning it for any signs of intrusion.

He held out his hand. "Allow me."

She dropped her keys into his palm, showing some signs of blistering, and stood aside. He unlocked the door and peered inside before shoving it wide.

She squeezed past him and entered the code to disarm the security system. "This turned into the longest dinner date ever."

"Dinner?" He slammed the door behind them and locked the dead bolt. "Wasn't that like twelve hours ago?"

"Practically. After you clean up, I'll heat up that pizza and we can finish it off. I think we deserve it."

He patted the thighs of his dirty jeans. "If these pants

look as bad in the back as they do in the front, I may have to trash them."

Fluffing her fingers through his straight, dark hair, she said, "You have ash in your hair, too. You're a total mess. You're welcome to take a shower here. I can toss your things into the washer."

His eyes met hers, and their smoldering darkness made her toes tingle. "And you?"

She glanced down at her grubby clothes. "I could do with a change of clothing, but you threw me out that window before the real fun began in that barn."

"Okay, which of the many numerous bathrooms should I use? The powder blue one? The forest green one? The…"

She drove her knuckle into his chest. "All right, all right. Don't be snarky. The guest room down from the main bedroom has a connecting bathroom, and I keep shower gel and shampoo in there. I'll grab you a towel from the linen closet in the hallway."

"Is it going to be warmed?" He shook his head. "Because if not…"

"You're pushing your luck here, Swain." She stepped around him to jog up the curved staircase. "While you're getting pretty, I'll dig through the Keldorf box some more to see if I can find any references to that pen in the barn."

He came up behind her. "And don't forget the pizza."

She reached the top of the stairs and pointed to the right of the landing. "Spare room's down there on the left. I'll find you a towel."

Jed gave her a mock salute and ambled down the hallway to the guest room.

Her heart skittered in her chest from her seeing him in this house again. When they'd been children, before they'd discovered their attraction to each other, he'd been a frequent guest here, as had most of the kids on the island. She was an only child, and her parents wanted to make sure she had lots of company. They started monitoring that company more closely when she hit her teen years, but she never imagined her father feared Jed enough to set him up for a crime he didn't commit.

As she grabbed the handle of the closet door, she glanced at her filthy hand. No point transferring dirt from her hand to Jed's towel. She did a pivot and ducked into the main bedroom, which she now occupied. The open door of the attached bath beckoned, and she slipped inside to wash her hands. She splashed some water on her face for good measure. She looked like a wreck.

She walked back out to the hallway and grabbed Jed a fresh towel from the stack on the shelf. He'd started his shower already but had left the bedroom door open for her, probably to grab his clothes, piled in a heap on the floor.

Clutching the towel to her chest, she crept toward the guest room and slipped inside. Jed hadn't been kidding about the bathrooms in different hues. If a bedroom had an attached bathroom, it mimicked the color scheme.

Hannah pulled her bottom lip between her teeth. Jed hadn't closed the bathroom door, either, and citrus-scented steam billowed into the bedroom.

She tiptoed to the open door and shouted without looking into the bathroom, "I have your towel. I'll toss it onto the rug."

She threw the towel into the space and took a peek to make sure it hit its target. It had landed on the other side of the toilet where he'd have to step out of the shower to reach it.

"Damn." She scurried into the bathroom to drape it over the rack on the wall outside the shower.

"Did you say something?" Jed turned to face the bathroom, his naked body on full display through the misty glass, his hands in his sudsy hair, his eyes closed against the shampoo.

Hannah tripped to a stop, the towel clutched to her chest as if she were the one missing clothes. Her mouth dropped open as she touched the shower door, a simple pane of glass between her and what she'd been dreaming about for the past eight years.

She must've made a noise because Jed ran a hand over his face and opened his eyes. They widened as he put his hand up to hers on the other side of the door.

She dropped the towel as if in a trance. Their eyes locked as she peeled off her clothes.

With the water streaming over his body, his hand still pressed to the glass, he watched her undress but didn't make a move.

Kicking her discarded clothes out of the way, she curled her fingers around the silver handle and pulled open the shower door. The steam curled around her hair, and droplets of water from the spray pinged her face.

Jed remained frozen, but his body betrayed how much he wanted her. She stepped into the shower and shivered. His large frame blocked the warm water from connecting with her skin but even though goose bumps pimpled her flesh, a fire burned in her belly, hotter than the blaze in the barn.

She reached out to him and smoothed her hands across his damp chest, his springy hair tickling her palms.

A soft groan escaped his lips. "Are you sure?"

In answer, her hands trailed down his wet body to his

erection. She took him in her hand and he gasped, wrapping one arm around her shoulders to urge her closer.

He planted a kiss on her mouth and turned to the side, the warm water from the showerhead hitting her body. He wrapped both arms around her and cupped her derriere in his hands, squeezing her soft flesh, resuming their kiss.

She stood on her tiptoes to trap his erection between her thighs, and he lifted her to help her reach the goal. She rocked her hips to rub her flesh against his hard shaft, throwing her head back as rivulets of pleasure coursed through her body.

Her knees weak, she could hardly stay upright and threw an arm to the side to brace her hand against the slippery tile.

He chuckled low in her ear. "You're going to bring us both down in here. Now I know why rich people have benches in their showers."

He walked her backward and eased her down on the granite bench that extended across one wall. Kneeling in front of her, he spread her legs open, and her breath hitched. He soaped up his hands and massaged the insides of her thighs as she dug her fingers into his shoulders.

She shuddered as he circled closer and closer to her swollen lips. He pinched them once, causing an electric shock to zing up her spine. Then he twisted around and lifted the second showerhead from its bracket. He aimed the spray between her legs, and her bottom hopped off the bench.

As he teased her with the water, she scraped her fingernails across his chest and whimpered, "Are we clean yet?"

"Clean?" he growled in her ear. "I thought you wanted to get dirty."

He hitched the showerhead back into place and replaced the water with his mouth. His tongue and lips sucked and caressed her until she cried out. For a moment, she felt suspended in space as elation suffused her body. She came back to earth as her orgasm clawed through her belly, waves of delight crashing through her over and over.

Drained but inspired, she wrapped her legs around his waist. "That was quite an introduction to Mr. Jed Swain."

"I thought I should make it worth your while, since you came in and…got all wet. Can I expect towel service like that all the time?" He gave her a chaste kiss at odds with his suggestive words.

"Of course." She ran a hand through his wet hair and squeezed it out. "Are we going to stay in here forever and turn into prunes? Because I think we have some unfinished business."

He closed his eyes as she tapped her fingertips along the length of him.

They abandoned the shower, both of them much cleaner than when they entered, and Jed swept up the towel from where she'd dropped it on the floor. As she stepped onto the rug, he wrapped her in the towel, rubbing his hands on her back to dry her off.

Tugging at the towel, she said, "This was supposed to be for you."

"You're the one who's shivering." He hoisted her in his arms and carried her into the adjoining room. He placed her on the edge of the bed. "Stay here."

She fell onto her back, grabbing at the covers. Her bed in the master was bigger than this one, but they didn't need a big bed. She wanted to stay as close to him as possible.

Several seconds later, Jed returned with another towel. He climbed on the bed, straddling her, and rubbed her with the towel in all the right places.

"Mmm." She ran her knuckles down his muscled thighs. "Who knew drying off could be so...sensuous."

Bracing himself with his elbows on either side of her, he kissed her forehead, eyelids, cheeks, ears, neck. "I'm glad you delivered that towel to me."

"I'm glad that shower door has see-through glass." She wrapped her legs around his hips.

He tucked a lock of hair behind her ear and smoothed his thumb along her cheek. "I don't have any, but do you have any...protection?"

Hannah swallowed. She'd been so carried away by her passion for Jed, she hadn't even considered using a condom. Someone had to be the responsible party here.

She said, "I have some condoms in my nightstand. We can just take this whole party over there."

He held up a finger as he scooted off the bed. "Stay right where you are. That main bedroom was your parents' room. I don't want to ruin the moment."

"Oh, please." She threw a pillow at him.

His ringing phone cut off his laugh. He crouched down and pulled the phone from his pocket. "It's Astrid. She's turned into my mother. Can you answer it?"

He unlocked the phone and tossed it to her as he turned to leave the room.

She tapped the cell. "Hi, Astrid. It's Hannah. Don't worry about Jed. He's with me...in every possible way."

Astrid drew in a soggy breath. "Hannah? Olly is gone. Someone kidnapped him...and left a dead bird in his bed."

Chapter Fourteen

Jed grabbed the box of condoms from the drawer next to Hannah's bed. The box was open, but Jed told himself not to count how many were left.

With the box clutched in his hand, he hurried back to the guest room down the hall where paradise awaited him. He burst into the room, shaking the box. "Success."

He tripped to a stop short of the bed as he caught sight of Hannah's pale face. She still had his cell phone pressed to her ear. Listening to Astrid on the other end with wide eyes, her hand over her heart.

He dropped the box on the bed. "What's wrong?"

"We'll be right there, Astrid. Wait for the police before going outside. Please."

Jed sat on the edge of the bed. "What's wrong with Astrid?"

"Someone kidnapped Olly. Did you know Tate was out of town?"

"He mentioned something, but I didn't think it was this soon." He dragged a hand through his wet hair. "Maybe Olly just snuck out. He's an adventurous boy as far as I can tell."

"Jed." She cupped his phone between both of her hands. "Someone left a dead bird on Olly's bed."

"What the hell?" He bounced from the bed and snatched up his soot-stained jeans from the floor. "She called the police?"

"She called the sheriff's department before she called you. I told her to stay put and wait for them, but I think she's going to go out to look for Olly. Maybe she's already been outside. It's dangerous for her to leave the house. He probably took Olly to lure her outside."

As Hannah voiced his every worry, Jed scrambled into his clothes, glad that Hannah had been too distracted to put them in the wash.

She rolled off the bed, dragging a towel behind her to cover up. "I'm coming with you. I told Astrid I'd be there."

When Hannah left the room, Jed jabbed at his phone and Astrid answered immediately. "Hannah and I are leaving in a few minutes. Are the police there yet?"

She sniffled. "Not yet. I don't trust them, Jed. My ex poisoned the Dead Falls Sheriff's Department against me. This could be Russ. I think Russ kidnapped Olly. He always threatened to take him from me."

Astrid didn't know the significance of the dead bird, and he wasn't about to tell her. Let her think it was her ex who took Olly for now.

"Maybe you can't trust the sheriff's department to investigate or find him, but you can trust them now to keep you safe."

"Keep me safe? What do I have to worry about? It's Olly who's in danger, and I'm going to find him."

"Astrid, you need to be there when the deputies arrive… and us, too. Just sit tight. We'll be there as soon as we can."

He ended the call and almost collided with Hannah in the

hallway. She had the luxury of changing into fresh clothes. Her damp hair hung in a slick ponytail over her shoulder.

"Astrid thinks this is her ex." He shook his head. "I didn't try to convince her otherwise."

"Russ? He's a cop in Seattle, isn't he? Why would he be leaving a dead bird in place of his son?"

"And I never told Astrid about the finches. The fewer people who know about that, the better."

She tugged at his sleeve. "Not knowing puts her in danger. We both know this killer isn't interested in the kids. It's the moms he wants."

They hustled downstairs, disrupting Siggy's napping place on the bottom step. Jed dragged the keys to his truck from his pocket. Although the air between them was fraught with tension, they didn't exchange another word until they were inside the truck with the engine running.

Throwing the truck into Drive, Jed said what they'd both been thinking. "Astrid is going to toss law enforcement's drug theory out the window."

"That's for sure. Astrid is squeaky clean. I don't think I've ever even seen her drunk, and we know Tate doesn't do drugs or have anything to do with the drug trade in this town. So, why target their house? Why target Astrid and her son?"

"She's a single mom, Hannah, just like the other two. This guy has something against single moms. Maybe he was raised by one."

"That could be a lot of people." She glanced at him out of the corner of her eye. "That could be you."

"Unfortunately, my dad didn't leave the house soon enough for that." Jed ground his back teeth together. "Why did this guy take Olly? What is the point of that? If he got into the house, why not just attack Astrid like all the others?"

"Maybe Olly saw him first." She clasped her hands in her lap. "I'm pretty sure the other kids didn't get a look at their moms' killer."

"I hope to God that's not the case." He slammed his hands against the steering wheel and then winced as his burned palms caused pain to shoot through his nerves. "I didn't even know Tate was leaving today. He should've told me."

"Then you really would've been torn." She smoothed a hand over his tensed forearm. "Stay with me after the fire at the barn or protect Astrid and Olly in Tate's absence? You can't be everywhere at once, Jed. Why would Tate expect that Astrid would need protection? The cops have been playing these murders as drug related. Most of the island breathes a sign of relief and thinks they're safe because they're not involved. Maybe that's why he started with the single moms who had substance abuse problems, leading the cops in one direction.

"If this is the same person who firebombed the barn, he must've headed straight to Astrid's after. What is he playing at? Why would he want a child?"

Hannah twisted her fingers in her lap. "Maybe Astrid's right. Maybe this is her ex, and the bird is a...coincidence."

"That's not good, either, but it's preferable to someone who has already killed twice snatching him." Jed aimed his truck toward the Mitchells' property.

He pointed to the revolving lights of the patrol car. "They beat us here. At least they're taking this seriously."

"A missing child on the heels of two murders? I would hope even Hopalong gets the significance."

Jed pulled up clear of the patrol car and jammed the truck

in Park. He jumped from the front seat and strode toward Astrid, her face pale in the moonlight.

He pulled her into a hug. "It's going to be okay. We'll find Olly."

She sobbed into his shoulder. "I don't know how he got out without my noticing."

Hannah came up behind Astrid and rubbed her back. "Did he leave on his own, or did someone break in?"

Wriggling from Jed's embrace, Astrid wiped her nose with the back of her hand. "Nobody broke in. I'm sure of it. The deputies checked the doors and windows. The dead bolt on the front door was unlocked. There's no key on the inside, so Olly must've walked out that way, but why? And where is he now?"

Hearing some yelling in the distance, Jed cocked his head. "Are the deputies out searching for him?"

"One is." She threw an arm behind her at the cabin. "The other one's in there looking for clues. If Russ were here, outside, and called to Olly, he'd come running. He knows his dad isn't the best father in the world, but he's the only one he's got."

"That's the way it goes." Jed smacked his hands together. "Olly has shown me a few of his favorite spots out in the woods. I'll check those."

Astrid covered her mouth. "I heard about that fire near the ramshackle house in Misty Hollow earlier. You don't think it has anything to do with Olly, do you?"

Jed shook his head. Obviously, Astrid had failed to notice his singed appearance in the dark. "I'm sure it doesn't."

"Maybe he just wandered off." Hannah squeezed Astrid's shoulder.

Jed raised his eyebrows at Hannah. He wandered off after

putting a dead finch on his pillow? Even if Astrid didn't see the significance of the bird, that theory probably wouldn't comfort her.

Hannah poked him in the back. "You go search those places. I'll stay here with Astrid."

Jed jogged back to his truck and retrieved a flashlight from the back seat. He then opened his toolbox in the truck bed and yanked out a pair of work gloves. If he was going to traipse through the wild, he needed to protect his hands from any more damage.

He waved one gloved hand at Astrid and Hannah and trooped into the forest, in a different direction from the deputy. As he cut a swath through the trees and bushes, his shoes cracking the twigs beneath them, he called Olly's name in a low voice. If the kid was scared, he probably wouldn't appreciate someone crashing through the woods and shouting his name.

His steps led him to the creek that rippled through this part of the forest, his heart heavy in his chest. That creek could get deep and fast in some parts, and he knew Olly liked to fish.

Jed tripped over a root and went down on one knee. He hoped he wasn't responsible for giving Olly any ideas about night fishing. He rose to his feet and brushed the leaves from his jeans. "Olly. Olly."

Jed froze, his ears cocked for a human sound amid the twittering and scuttling of the night creatures. The sound of rushing water gave him pause.

"Olly." Jed took two steps forward and stopped again. This time he heard a squeak that sounded more boy than rodent. "Olly, you there? It's Jed."

A sigh and a scuffle answered him, and Jed crept toward

the source. He patted the empty pocket of his jacket. He should've brought his piece. What if this was some kind of trap? What if someone was holding Olly hostage?

A shadow by the creek moved, and Jed ducked behind a tree. He peered around the trunk, his gaze drawn to a light dancing in the air. As his eyes adjusted to the gloom, he made out the figure of a boy—Olly—holding his cell phone. He knew Astrid had caved and allowed him a phone for emergencies only. This counted.

Jed's gaze flicked to the right and left of Olly, but the boy seemed to be alone. He emerged from behind the tree and took a cautious step forward. "Olly?"

Olly spun around and dropped his phone. "Oh, h-hi, Jed."

Jed eased out a breath. "What are you doing out here, buddy?"

Olly bent forward, scooped up his phone and dropped it in the pocket of his hoodie. "Nothing."

"Doesn't look like nothing." Jed swept the beam of his light across Olly's body. The boy looked fine—just guilty.

"I'm just looking for a good nighttime fishing spot…you know, like you told me."

Jed's heart sank. It was his fault…but what about that bird?

"Yeah, well, you need to tell your mom first, or better yet, have her come with you. She's worried about you, dude."

"Oh." Olly rocked back and forth on his feet. "She wasn't supposed to know."

"Moms have a way of knowing everything." Jed held the flashlight beneath his chin to create a ghoulish face. "Come back with me and you can tell your mom all about it, so she won't be worried anymore."

Olly cracked a smile and shuffled through the dirt, leaves and twigs toward Jed.

"You okay? You hurt?" Jed knew there was more to Olly's story, but he didn't want to rush him.

"Hurt?" Olly hopped over a felled log. "No."

"Okay, just checking. Anyone come out here with you?" Jed slid a glance to the side.

Olly shook his head back and forth so vigorously, his shaggy blond hair whipped back and forth. "No."

Jed had learned to pick up on deception from cons—the most practiced liars on the planet. He had no trouble discerning this bald-faced fib.

"Okay." Jed led the way back to Astrid. When they emerged from the forest, Jed called out, "Got him. Olly, Olly, all come free."

Astrid let out a yelp and ran toward them. She grabbed Olly and squeezed the breath out him. Then she shook him a little. "Where were you? Why'd you sneak out at night and go into the forest?"

Bending his head, Olly scuffed the toe of his sneaker in the dirt. "Just checking out a fishing spot."

"At midnight?" Astrid wedged a hand on her hip. "Why would you do that? What was with the dead bird on your bed? Did you think that was funny?"

Jed exchanged a look with Hannah and held his breath.

"Yeah, that's it. Just a joke." With his head still tipped forward, Olly spoke to his feet.

"Oh, no you don't." Astrid wedged a knuckle beneath Olly's chin and tilted up his head. "You tell me what's going on right now."

"Nothing, Mom." Olly's bottom lip jutted forward.

Astrid wasn't having it. She thrust out her hand, palm up. "Let me see your phone."

"Mom." Olly's voice took on a whining quality known to parents around the world.

"Now, young man." She wiggled her fingers.

Olly dug the cell phone he'd been looking at when Jed spied him out of his pocket and dropped it into his mom's hand.

Astrid knew the password and punched it in. The light from the phone illuminated her face, set in hard lines, as she scrolled through Olly's text messages.

The two deputies had heard Jed and now stood just outside the circle of him, Hannah, Astrid and Olly, looking on with relief and curiosity.

Through clenched teeth, Astrid said, "I told you not to communicate with your father secretly."

Hannah nudged Jed, and he shrugged. Could this all really be a coincidence?

Astrid stabbed a button on the phone and listened. "No voice mail. If your father is communicating with you on a burner phone, you know that's not normal, right?"

"Wait, what?" Jed's gaze dropped to the phone in Astrid's hands. "How do you know that's Russ?"

"Because he identifies himself." She turned the phone, screen out, and tilted it back and forth. "He contacted Olly earlier and told him he had a nighttime fishing spot to show him. Told him not to tell me and, probably in an attempt to terrify me, asked him to put a dead bird on his bed."

Jed's heart slammed against his chest so hard, his ribs rattled. "Are you kidding? Did you see your father when you came outside, Olly?"

"No." He chewed on his bottom lip. "He left me the bird

on the porch. I put it on my bed and then ran outside, but it wasn't to scare you, Mom."

Astrid tapped the phone's display. "He texted Olly the directions to the fishing spot, indicating he'd meet him there because he couldn't risk being seen by me. So, he's not only sneaking around, encouraging Olly to lie to me, he's putting him in danger by having him traipse through the forest at night on his own."

Jed placed his hand on the boy's slumped shoulder. "Did you see your dad down by the creek?"

"No." Olly sniffed. "I was waiting for him, but you showed up instead."

Astrid grabbed Hannah's arm. "Hannah, can you take Olly inside and see if he needs anything?"

"Be happy to. C'mon, Olly."

When the two of them disappeared into the cabin, Astrid pulled out her own phone and tapped it. This time someone must've picked up on the other end. "What the hell are you doing, Russ? Where are you? How dare you lure Olly out into the night?"

A voice loud enough for Jed to hear responded over the line. "What are you talking about? I'm working right now in Seattle. I haven't spoken to Olly since the last time you allowed it. If you don't believe me, call my sergeant. Better yet, here's my partner."

Russ's partner spoke more softly and Jed couldn't hear what he said, but looking at Astrid's face told him all he needed to know.

Russ didn't lure Olly out of the house at midnight, instructing him to leave a dead finch on his pillow...but someone did.

Chapter Fifteen

By the time Jed drove Hannah back to the house, he'd convinced her that the killer, pretending to be Russ Crockett, had lured Olly out to the woods. They just couldn't figure out why.

"How did he get Olly's cell phone number?"

Jed shrugged. "I'm sure that wouldn't be too hard to do. Do you think this guy tried to entice the other children into going outside?"

"If he did, neither one mentioned it to me." Hannah hugged her purse to her chest. "But why Astrid? She's not into drugs. She doesn't hang out with the same people as Zoey and Stephanie did."

"Seattle PD has to see that this is related to those dead birds—and the Keldorf property." Jed rubbed his eyes.

They hadn't budged from Jed's truck since he pulled it into her drive, even though they both needed rest after the day they'd had. "But Seattle homicide didn't even come out to question Astrid. Do you think it's because they don't want to let the public know about the birds? I mean, Astrid doesn't have a clue, and I didn't want to be the one to tell her."

"They're going to have to tell her if they plan to question

her properly. She may have connections to the other women that we don't know about."

Hannah gave him a sharp glance. "You're going to tell her tonight, aren't you?"

"I don't want to scare her any more than she already is, but she needs to know, and we need to know if she has any links to Zoey or Stephanie. I'll just be giving her a heads-up, anyway. I'm sure Detective Chu is going to question her in relation to the other homicides. How can he not? They can't ignore those birds any longer. They can't ignore the fire tonight."

"Last night." She tapped the number glowing on the dash of his truck. "It's morning."

He ran a hand through his tangled hair. "Are you going to be okay here?"

"I'll be fine. I'm not a single mother." She cracked open the door of the truck. "Get back to Astrid and Olly. What you tell her is going to terrify her."

He walked her to the front door and cupped her face with both of his hands. "What happened earlier…"

"Was amazing." She put a finger to his lips. "Let's just leave it at that. No analysis or Monday morning quarterbacking."

He kissed her fingertip and then kissed her mouth. "Okay, deal. Set your security system, and I'll get you that ammo tomorrow…today."

"Will do."

Jed stayed right on her porch until she locked up inside. Parting the curtains at the front window, she waved as he backed out of her drive.

She wandered into the guest bedroom, gathered the damp

towels and straightened the covers on the bed. She picked up the condom box and took it back to her bedroom.

As she sat on the edge of her bed, Siggy jumped up beside her, his motor running strong.

She leaned across him and tossed the box in the drawer of her nightstand. "We definitely need to stock up on those."

AT HER APPOINTMENT with Sheldon the next day, Hannah tried every which way to wheedle more details from him about the night his mom was murdered. He gave no hint at all that anyone lured him outside or that he left the trailer at all.

What the hell had happened at Astrid's last night? Why would the killer want to get Olly out of the cabin? Olly was older than the other two kids, so maybe the killer was afraid he'd wake up during the murder.

After Sheldon's session, Hannah returned to her house and collapsed on the sofa with a file from the Keldorf case in her hands. She shuffled through some of the statements from the surviving foster kids.

They never had any complaints about Chet Keldorf or his wife, Sheila. They said he did get sad sometimes and wanted to be alone, and Chet's brother, Nate, indicated that Chet had suffered from depression for a number of years and may have had other issues. Did something just click in his head one day? Family annihilators often showed no signs of mental illness or violent behavior before the incident. Keldorf could've fallen into that category.

She dug a little deeper into the files. Why would her father hang on to this case? It could just be because it was the biggest of his career, even though he'd been a lowly deputy at the time.

The pages that detailed Chet's suicide, the final shot fired that day, bled red with her father's margin notes and question marks. She turned the pages this way and that, squinting at her father's scribbles.

Chet had delivered the suicide shot by placing the shotgun under his chin, not an uncommon way to kill yourself with a shotgun. It's not like you could hold it to your temple. But her father had circled the details of the other wounds on Chet's body. Keldorf had a lump on the back of his head. The coroner had Indicated that this could've come from the rock he'd hit when he fell over. Her father seemed to be questioning this finding. Did he believe someone else had delivered that blow and set the scene for a murder-suicide?

Hannah ran her finger down another page to locate the info for Chet's brother, Nate. He lived in Seattle at the time of the killings. Was he still there? It might be worth talking to him today to find out what he remembered. Jed had mentioned this yesterday.

Her cell phone on the table rang, and Hannah jumped. It seemed she only needed to think about Jed to conjure him up.

"How's Astrid?" She shoved the file folder from her lap and curled one leg beneath her.

"She's fine. I told her our suspicions, and she's heading off the island for a few days, at least until Tate returns."

"Did the police question her?" Siggy wedged his furry body next to her thigh, and she scratched him behind the ears.

"They did. She said they asked her the same things I asked her, and she gave them the same answers. She doesn't do drugs, knew both women only peripherally and didn't hang with the same crowd. Zoey's ex, Chase, came on to her once or twice, but she shut him down pretty quickly and she said he ignored her after that."

"Were the police able to trace the phone that called Olly's?"

"Burner. Now out of service."

"Of course. And the bird? Did they acknowledge the significance of the dead finch?"

"They did. Said it was obviously the guy's calling card or something, but they haven't necessarily connected it to the Keldorf crime."

"Really?" Siggy flattened his ears at her sharp tone and sprang off the couch. "Even after we were almost burned alive in that barn last night?"

"Yeah, about that."

She planted both feet on the floor and leaned forward. "What does that mean?"

"I got the impression that Seattle thinks we're trying to insert ourselves into this case for some reason—maybe to keep suspicion off me."

"Off you?" Hannah wanted to throw the phone across the room. Instead, she gripped it so hard, it dug into her palm. "Aren't they satisfied with your alibi yet?"

"They thought it was unusual that one of the people who provided my alibi also happened to be a target of this killer."

"So, we tossed a Molotov cocktail into the barn ourselves?" She ground her teeth together. "Is Seattle Homicide as incompetent as our own sheriff's department?"

Jed blew out a noisy breath. "You're asking the wrong person, but Astrid did tell me something interesting before she left."

"Oh?"

"She said that Olly broke his wrist several months ago and his doctor reported it to Child Protective Services because Olly had some suspicious bruising on his wrist, and Astrid had been reported to CPS before."

"Astrid? No way. She's not neglectful."

"She's pretty sure the previous anonymous report came from her ex, so she wasn't that steamed about it, but get this. In casual conversation with Stephanie Boyd one night, Stephanie complained that the same doc had reported her to CPS. He's Dr. Robbins. I think you mentioned he was seeing Sheldon, too. He may be a connection among the three women."

"Oh, my God. Dr. Robbins is the physician who treated Sheldon when he came in after the murder. I haven't received Chrissy Boyd's complete files yet, but I'll bet that report to CPS is in there." Hannah put a hand to her throat. "Do you think Dr. Robbins might have something to do with this? Maybe he thinks he's protecting the kids."

"Strange way to protect them, but it's a link—one the cops don't know about yet because Astrid didn't mention it to them."

Hannah glanced at the time on her phone before answering Jed. "I have loads of reasons for talking to Dr. Robbins. I'll start this afternoon. Also, you mentioned Chet Keldorf's brother, Nate. I think we need to talk to him, too."

"Did you find out anything else about him?"

"Not him, but my father's notes are questioning whether Chet's death was really a suicide. Nate may be able to shed more light on his brother's state of mind."

"I can use my PI connections to get a line on Nate Keldorf. You talk to the doc, and then we'll compare notes."

"This feels…right." She bit her bottom lip while she listened to Jed breathe across the line. If she'd worked with him eight years ago, would she have been able to help him avoid conviction for a crime he didn't commit?

"I'll call you later…and be careful."

Hannah cupped the phone between her hands after Jed ended the call. She'd been careful all her life. Maybe it was time to take some risks.

Chapter Sixteen

After a sandwich and another patient, Hannah drove to the hospital. She had a million and one reasons to talk to Dr. Robbins, so none of her questions should seem strange or out of bounds. Her knees bounced anyway, and she almost dropped her phone when the doctor's nurse called her name.

Becky, Dr. Robbins's nurse, smiled at her, as she widened the door. "He's in between patients right now and can give you a few minutes."

"Thanks, Becky." She followed Becky in her flowered smock and pink crocs down the hall. Dr. Robbins's pediatric medicine office followed the same decor as her own office for children—plenty of bright colors and cheerful artwork.

Becky left her at the open door of Robbins's office, and Hannah rapped on it to draw the doctor's attention away from his computer screen.

It worked. He glanced up and lowered his glasses to the tip of his nose. "Hello, Hannah. Sit down and excuse the sandwich."

"Even doctors have to eat. Sorry to interrupt your lunch, Dr. Robbins."

"Bob. Call me Bob." He waved the sandwich in the air and a thread of lettuce dropped to his blotter.

She settled into the chair across the desk from the genial-faced doctor. "Have you heard about the attempted kidnapping of Astrid Mitchell's son, Olly?"

"I did hear something about that. She didn't bring Olly in for a checkup, so I'm assuming he's okay." He took a bite of his sandwich and dabbed the lettuce with the tip of his finger.

"He's fine. He thought it was his dad luring him outside, and in the end, nothing happened to either Astrid or Olly."

He nodded and patted his mouth with a napkin. "That's good to hear. Do the police think this is related to the two murders? As far as I know, Astrid Mitchell is not an addict, and she takes good care of her son."

Hannah's pulse ticked up. "Why did you add that?"

He put down his sandwich and dusted the crumbs from his fingers. "Look, we're both professionals and we're working with the same kids. I don't think I have to tell you that the Grady boy and the Boyd girl were mistreated."

"Mistreated? You think there was abuse?"

"Definite abuse in the Grady household. The Boyd situation is one of neglect due to the mother's addictions."

"And yet you reported Astrid Mitchell to CPS—just like you reported the other two." She was just throwing that out there—that he'd reported Zoey, too. She didn't know that for sure.

His nod confirmed her suspicions. "I did. For his broken wrist and some bruises on his arm. I didn't really think there had been any abuse, but Astrid was in the system due to some bogus charges by an ex. I didn't know that at the time, saw the initial report and contacted CPS about the broken wrist."

"That's not fair." Heat rushed to Hannah's cheeks, and her fingers curled around the arms of the chair.

He held up his hands. "I know, but the charge hadn't been expunged yet. I was just doing my duty as mandate reported. You would have, too."

She relaxed her grip. "You're right, but now we have a situation where three women who had CPS reports against them have been targeted by a killer."

His dark, bushy brows shot up. "Do the police know for sure that Olly's mystery man is related to the two murders?"

"Th-there was some other evidence at the scene that points to it, but now that we know all three were in the system, it becomes clear."

"Or it's a coincidence." He picked up his sandwich. "As you know, child neglect often goes hand in hand with substance abuse issues. It could still be a case of drug deals gone wrong, and the kids are collateral damage—as they often are."

She scooted to the edge of her chair and leaned over his desk. "But that's not Astrid, is it?"

"We know that." He waved his mustard-smudged finger between the two of them. "Maybe he's just trying to throw the cops off his scent. He didn't harm Astrid, did he? And it sounds like he had the chance."

"I was thinking about that." She rubbed her chin with her knuckle. "Astrid was outside, on her own. He could've killed her then, just like the other two."

"But he didn't."

Drumming her fingers on Robbins's desk, she said, "Could it be someone who has access to those CPS files? Maybe he's making his way down the list. Perhaps he realized Astrid didn't fit the profile."

"Sounds like a theory for those detectives. I'm not saying those two women got what they deserved, but their children might have a better future without them. Parents have responsibilities." Robbins pursed his lips as he pushed his half-eaten sandwich away from him and straightened his computer monitor. "I'm sorry, Hannah. I have to get back to work before I see my next patient."

"Of course." She pushed back from the chair so fast, she had to save it from falling over. "Thanks for your time and input."

She hustled out of the office with a quick wave to Becky and the receptionist.

When she made it outside, she called Jed.

"Everything okay, Hannah?"

"Yeah, but I just got a seriously weird vibe from Dr. Robbins."

"Weird vibe? You don't suspect him, do you?"

"No, that would be crazy, right? But he practically said Sheldon and Chrissy might be better off without their moms."

"That's a strange thing for a doctor to admit, especially a pediatrician, but he probably sees some things the rest of us don't even want to think about."

"It was odd, but he did cop to reporting Zoey to CPS, as well as Stephanie and Astrid."

"Why'd he tag Astrid? She'd never hurt Olly."

"Something about a ding on her record before, from her ex, that required him to report her again for Olly's broken wrist and bruises."

"That report was false." Jed clipped his words.

"Robbins said he knew that now, but that it hadn't been removed from the record when he checked it several months ago."

"I guess I'm not the only one on this island who's suffered from false accusations. What are you going to do with the information?”

“I’m going to tell Detective Chu that all three women were in the CPS system. It’s a strong link. The drug theory applies only to Zoey and Stephanie.”

“He killed only Zoey and Stephanie. We still don’t know what that was all about last night with Astrid and Olly.”

“That’s exactly what Robbins said.”

“He’s not wrong. That dead bird on Olly’s bed could’ve been a hoax, maybe some teenagers. We already know that piece of info is circulating out there.”

“What a horrible joke to play on someone, but it can’t be teens. It was too sophisticated. Whoever planned it knew Olly’s cell phone number, went to the trouble of buying a burner phone and knew about Russ and the divorce.”

“It’s a small island, Hannah.”

“I’m still bringing it to Detective Chu.” She took a deep breath of sea-scented air. “What have you been up to?”

“Besides getting Astrid and Olly the hell out of Dodge? I tracked down Nate Keldorf.”

“Yes!” She pumped her fist, startling a pedestrian on his phone. “Is he still in Seattle?”

“He’s on Whidbey Island now. He owns a liquor store.”

“Your sources are very good. Did you call him?”

“Not yet. I’d rather see him in person. I don’t want him giving us the runaround.”

“At least we’re not cops. He must be sick of cops.” She paused as she stepped off the curb. “You did say us, didn’t you? Give us the runaround?”

“I sure did. Are you free to take a trip out to Whidbey tonight?”

“Of course.” She glanced down at her work clothes. “Just need to head home and change.”

An hour later, Jed pulled in front of her house, his truck idling behind her car. She gave Siggy a quick pat before slamming the door behind her and rushing down the drive. They had to hurry to catch the last ferry from Dead Falls to Whidbey. Jed had arranged a private boat for the trip back. Independent boat owners did a brisk service, ferrying between the islands, but those boaters always had to be on the lookout for drug dealers and mules transporting drugs to Canada.

Hannah slid into the truck beside Jed. She plucked at his black T-shirt and then pointed to hers. "Matching outfits."

"You're starting to dress like a PI."

"I'm learning from the best." She winked at him.

"Yeah, I haven't solved much of anything on this case." He wheeled the truck onto the road and headed toward the harbor on the other side of the island.

"I think we're making more headway than the cops." Cupping her hands around her eyes, she said, "They have tunnel vision about this drug thing."

"You can't blame them. Sheriffs and police departments have to do things by the book. I hate to say it, but that's why your father was so successful. He broke the rules." He held up a hand. "That's also why he was so corrupt."

Hannah shifted in her seat. "Let's just concentrate on Nate Keldorf for now. He was the younger brother. I think Chet had a good fifteen years on him. Second marriage, I believe."

"You've done your homework." Jed coughed and pounded his chest. "I'm still feeling the effects of that fire, you?"

"You got the brunt of that, but you're lucky the flames didn't spread any faster while you were chopping at the wall of the barn with that axe. That pen we saw in the barn—"

she rubbed her palms against the thighs of her jeans "—one of that was left after the fire. I checked with a friend of mine who's on the volunteer firefighting squad."

"You think there was a person or persons locked in that pen, don't you?"

"Don't you? Someone scratched out words on the wall. That was no pig."

"And someone didn't want us investigating in that barn too closely."

"Who would still care about that after all these years if it didn't have some significance for today?"

"Maybe Keldorf can help us." Jed propped his hand on top of the steering wheel, leveling a finger straight ahead. "There's the ferry. We made it. I have our tickets on my phone."

The sun sank into Discovery Bay on the ninety minute ride to Whidbey, and they stepped onto a dark island when they disembarked with other passengers hurrying to their destinations.

Jed had the address of Keldorf's liquor store and entered it into an app on his phone to order a car. The car arrived in less than ten minutes for the short ride to their destination.

Hannah blew out a sigh of relief when she saw the lights on at NB Liquors and Convenience. She tapped on the glass. "What do you think the NB stands for?"

The driver heard her and answered, "That's Nate Bradley's place."

They exited the car and stood on the sidewalk facing the store, the yellow neon from the sign giving Jed's face an orange glow.

Hannah said, "Nate Bradley Keldorf. You can't blame him for changing his last name."

"That's for sure. That story must've been national news at the time."

They hovered at the entrance until the lone customer in the store left, carrying a six-pack and a bag of chips.

Jed touched her back. "Ready?"

"Let's ruin Nate Keldorf's evening." She rolled her shoulders as Jed ushered her through the door first.

A middle-aged man glanced up from behind the counter, the silver in his hair catching the light, the lines on his face etched deeply around his mouth and eyes. "Hello, folks."

Jed nodded while Hannah returned Nate's greeting. As they approached the counter, Nate gripped the edge as if bracing for bad news. Had he already sensed their mission?

When he reached the counter, Jed stuck his hand out. "I'm Jed Swain and this is Hannah Maddox. We'd like to ask you a few questions about your brother, Chet Keldorf, and the crime."

Nate dropped Jed's hand in the middle of the shake and his face blanched as he took a step back, his shoulders meeting the rack of cigarettes behind him. "Who are you? Why are you here? Did *he* send you?"

Jed lifted his hands. "Hey, we're not here to cause any trouble for you. We've had a couple of murders out on Dead Falls Island. My buddy's sister was a victim, and he asked to me do some snooping around. I've just seen some…links to the murder scene at your brother's house."

"Links?" Nate brought a shaky hand to his face and covered his eyes for a second. "I've heard about those murders. Everyone here has, but my brother didn't kill any young women."

Hannah licked her lips. "I'm working as a forensic psychologist with the Seattle PD, Mr. K—Nate. I'm just curious what you think about your brother and what drove him to do it."

Nate's faded blue eyes gazed over her shoulder. "My brother was a lot of things, but he wasn't a killer."

Hannah's pulse jumped. "You don't believe he killed his family and himself?"

"No." Nate picked at the label of a basket of lighters on the counter with his thumbnail.

"You said he was a lot of things." Jed narrowed his eyes. "What kinds of things?"

Studying the sticky paper on his nail, Nate said, "Those kids he was always fostering?" He flicked the paper onto the counter. "He wasn't doing that out of the goodness of his heart."

Knots formed in Hannah's belly, and she felt sick. "What do you mean by that?"

"I mean…" Nate jerked back when a couple of rowdy twentysomethings stumbled into the store.

Jed braced his hands on the counter and leaned forward. "Who do you think killed your brother's family and your brother, Nate?"

Nate's gaze darted to the two men discussing the merits of light beer with the refrigerator door propped open. He whispered, "Come back in an hour at closing. I'll leave the door unlocked."

One of the men called across the store, "Hey, Nate. You got any of this IPA cold?"

Nate gave Jed one last look before leaving his station behind the counter. "I thought I put a case on the bottom shelf at the end of the row here."

As Jed and Hannah turned, a couple walked through the door holding hands. They squeezed past them and parked on the sidewalk.

"What was that all about?" Hannah paced a few yards and spun around to pace back to Jed. "My father suggested the same thing in his case notes. Keldorf wasn't the killer. Someone set him up to take the fall and then killed him."

Jed jerked his thumb over his shoulder. "It sounds like Nate has his suspicions. Did you hear what he said when he found out we were there about the murders? He asked if *he* sent us. Who the hell is this 'he'?"

"Hopefully, he'll tell us that at closing time." She chewed on the side of her thumb. "Do you think his brother harmed the foster children? Do you think he kept them penned up as punishment?"

"That's sickening to imagine, but it might give someone a motive."

"But to kill the two foster children, as well? How is that rescuing them?" Hannah folded her arms over her queasy stomach as she stepped aside for a few more people entering Nate's liquor store.

Taking her arm, Jed said, "I'm hungry. Can we get something to eat while we wait?"

"I'm not sure I have much of an appetite, but we need to kill time." She rubbed her belly.

Nate's store enjoyed a bounty of foot traffic, situated as it was on a hopping street with several bustling restaurants and shops. Jed led her to one of the many eating establishments, still boasting outdoor patios in the front to catch the last wisps of summer before the fall chill moved in.

They nabbed the last table on the patio, and Hannah snatched a menu from the table as she plopped into the hard chair. "Nate obviously feels the same way my father did—Chet wasn't responsible for that carnage. Maybe the person who was is responsible for Zoey and Stephanie. But what's the connection?"

"The kids." Jed trailed a finger down the plastic menu. "Are you eating?"

"The kids. But why? Sheldon and Chrissy aren't foster kids."

"They might be now, if a family member doesn't step up."

"So, why would the killer want to send more kids into the system? And why kill those Keldorf fosters?"

"Let's wait to see what Nate has to say first. I think it's a coup we got this far with him. The police obviously haven't questioned him yet." Jed gave an encouraging smile to the approaching waitress.

Her eyes brightened when they focused on Jed, and she asked, "Are you ready to order?"

Hannah studied Jed's face for a second for signs of flirtation but saw only businesslike politeness—another way prison had changed him. He'd always had a charming side that set the girls buzzing. That's why she'd held off for so long on upgrading him from friend to boyfriend status. She didn't want to be like all those other girls who fell at his feet. Now he had a reserve around women—even her.

"Hey, you." Jed waved the menu in her face. "Do you want something to eat?"

She started, her cheeks warming. "Just an iced tea for me, thanks."

Jed ordered fish and chips and thanked the waitress curtly. Then he tucked away both menus and spread his hands on the table, his thumbs meeting. "You're not gonna let this go, are you?"

"I don't want to ruin your dinner."

"Nothing ruins my appetite." He tapped one of his fingers, still on the table. "One of the bio parents of a Keldorf foster kid finds out Chet isn't the kindly father figure he pretends to be. He—or she…or both—heads to the Keldorf property, maybe even sees that human pen, and goes off. Kills the family—Keldorf because he's evil, mom because she didn't do anything to stop the evil and then maybe the two young ones to spare them more abuse or maybe just to get rid of witnesses."

Hannah shivered. "Go on. Why'd he leave the older two foster kids?"

"Because they belonged to him. Those were his kids, and he was protecting them from the Keldorfs."

She nodded vigorously, her chin almost touching her chest. "Sets it up as a murder-suicide and gets away with it. Now thirty years later, in his fifties, he comes back to Dead Falls to…rescue other kids from crummy situations? We can acknowledge that both Sheldon and Chrissy were neglected. Maybe he's trying to save them from that neglect, putting them with other family members. They do both have relatives. They don't need to go into the system, as long as these family members are interested in taking them."

"Could be." He thanked the beaming waitress for their teas. "The dead finches are a nod to the Keldorf crime, tying them together."

She dumped some sweetener into her tea. "We need to find out who the survivors of the Keldorf massacre were."

"I think Nate Keldorf can help with that. Maybe he already knows it's one of those parents."

Hannah slumped in her seat. "This is just starting to make a little sense."

She made an effort to change the subject and by the time Jed's food arrived, his golden fries and beer-battered fish made her mouth water.

Jed reached for the ketchup and squirted a big puddle onto his plate. He dragged a couple of fries through the red goop, and his hand froze halfway to his mouth. "You want some of this, don't you?"

Lodging her tongue in the corner of her mouth, Hannah dropped her gaze from the fries pinched between Jed's fingers to the black T-shirt fitted across the expanse of his chest. "I want all of it."

"Don't get greedy." He stuffed the fries into his mouth and swallowed, his eyes widening. "Wait, are we still talking about food?"

"Sort of." She pointed to his plate.

"Help yourself. There's a piece of fish here with your name on it, too." He waved his hand in the air to get the waitress's attention as she dropped a check at the next table.

"Everything okay?" The waitress gave him a big smile.

"Can we get an extra plate? My girlfriend changed her mind."

The waitress's smile faded a little, but she rallied. "Of course. I can get you some extra fries to share, too. On the house."

"She's nice." Jed shoved his plate toward Hannah. "In the meantime, help yourself."

Hannah snorted as she picked out a few fries, avoiding

the glob of ketchup. "She's nice because she likes you. Isn't that why you called me your girlfriend? To fend her off?"

"Fend her off? Is that what I was doing?" He plunged a fork into his coleslaw. "I didn't know she needed fending."

"If you were so oblivious to her obvious fascination with you, why'd you go for the girlfriend move?" Hannah dabbed her lips primly with her napkin.

"Didn't even realize I'd said it. Came naturally. Does it bother you?"

"Not at all." Hannah glanced up at the smitten waitress when she returned with a plate of fries in her hand. "Thanks."

"Of course. Anything else?" She tried to focus on Hannah, but she finally gave up and grinned at Jed.

He answered for both of them. "We're good, thanks a lot."

"I'm curious." Hannah shoved the fries to one side of the plate and stabbed a piece of fish with her fork, launching it over to her plate. "Do you always get such good service at restaurants or just when you have enthusiastic female waitresses?"

Jed cocked his head as he chewed. "Not sure. I never seem to have any complaints about service."

"I'll bet you don't."

Putting aside thoughts of their true mission here on Whidbey, Hannah managed to eat all the extra french fries and Jed's third piece of fish. When she finished off her tea refill, she sat back and sighed. "I needed that. I hadn't eaten since an early lunch."

"You can't investigate on an empty stomach." He glanced at his phone. "You ready? It's closing time at NB Liquors."

"Let's see what Nate has to say about his brother and

those foster kids." She reached for her purse, but Jed had already snapped down his card.

"Don't forget to leave her a nice tip." She tapped his plastic with her fingertip.

Jed signed off on a generous tip for the waitress, and they made their way back to the liquor store.

They paused outside. Nate had turned out a few lights and had put the closed sign on the door. Peering inside the window, Hannah said, "I don't see him behind the counter. Do you think he changed his mind and closed up on us?"

"He said he'd leave the door unlocked." Jed grabbed the handle of the glass door and yanked it open. "And he did."

He held the door open for her, and she walked into the store, her head on a swivel. "Where is he?"

Jed approached the counter. "Mr. Bradley? Nate?"

Hannah joined him and then grabbed his arm. "Those boxes weren't like that before."

"Are you sure?" Jed's body vibrated next to hers, as if the toppled over boxes had put him on high alert.

They'd put her on high alert, too, and the hair on the back of her neck vibrated. "Nate?"

"Stay right here." Jed brushed past her and skirted around the end of the counter.

Hannah had no intention of being left behind. She followed him, her hip colliding with the edge of the counter.

Jed tripped to a stop at the entrance to the back room of the store, his arms stretched to the sides, his hands braced against the frame.

Hannah plowed into his back, and then ducked beneath one of his arms to see what made him stop suddenly.

She wished she hadn't. She balled her fist and shoved it

against her mouth as she took in the body of Nate Keldorf, sprawled in the back of his liquor store, a knife protruding from his chest.

Chapter Seventeen

Jed made a grab for Hannah too late. A squeak came from the back of her throat, and she listed to the side.

He grabbed her shoulders from behind and pulled her back, toward him, toward the store. "Stay out of the blood. I'll check his pulse. Get on the phone."

His staccato voice seemed to snap her out of a trance. Her collapsing frame suddenly straightened, and she took a step back. She dug for her phone as he crept forward, avoiding the puddle of blood as it lazily meandered farther and farther from Nate's body.

Jed placed two fingers against the side of Nate's neck. A feeble pulse trembled beneath his fingers. "He's still alive, Hannah. Tell the 911 operator."

As Hannah spoke on the phone, Jed leaned in close toward Nate's lips, which had cracked open. Jed whispered, "Who did this, Nate?"

The man's eyelids fluttered, and a bubble of blood formed at his mouth.

Jed put his ear closer to the dying man's lips. "Say it, Nate. Who attacked you?"

Nate's mouth gaped like a fish a few times, and then he growled out, "Ad, ad."

"Ad? Adam? Adam who?"

The effort proved too much for Nate, and he lost consciousness, his mouth slack, more blood trickling from the corner.

Jed scooped a T-shirt with the liquor store's name on it from a box and used it to apply pressure to the bloody wound from which Nate's life force was slowly leaking.

Hannah hovered above him. "Is he still alive?"

"He's gone."

"Ambulance is on the way." A wail of sirens from the street punctuated Hannah's words, and she spun around. "I'll direct them back here."

When the EMTs arrived, Jed finally scooted away from the body, leaving the blood-soaked T-shirt still bunched in Nate's midsection.

Once the ambulance arrived, the floodgates opened. The cops arrived, and a crowd of people followed in their wake, their heads bobbing outside the front windows, trying to get a peek.

Jed and Hannah dealt with the cops' questions, Hannah giving him a sharp look when he told them that Nate had named Ad as the culprit with what would probably be his dying breaths.

They also referred the Whidbey officers to Detective Howard Chu, letting them know the knife attack on Nate could be related to the murders on Dead Falls Island.

After another hour of grilling, the cops let them leave the store. They slipped into a dark bar across the street, where Jed scrubbed at Nate's bloodstains on his shirt.

Hannah ordered a glass of wine while Jed got a glass of water, hoping to rinse the metallic taste of blood from his mouth.

Hannah took two long slugs from her glass and planted her elbows on the bar. "Who the hell is Ad and how did he get to Nate? How'd he know we were here? Did someone follow us from the ferry?"

Jed sucked down his second glass of water and tapped the mahogany surface of the bar for another. "How'd he know we were at the Keldorf place?"

"I don't understand how we could've been followed there and here—not that I was looking for a tail. Were you?"

"I should've been after the fire at the Keldorf barn."

Jed rolled the glass between his hands, wiping away the moisture on the outside with his palms. The chill reached his spine. "Unless he's not tailing us."

"What do you mean?" Hannah downed the rest of her wine in one gulp.

"He showed up at the Keldorf property after we did. He manages to get to Whidbey Island and knows about Nate Keldorf and his liquor store. He didn't have to be following us. He could have a tracker on one of us."

Hannah's fingers curled around the stem of her wineglass, her knuckles white. "How?" Then something dawned on her. "We took your truck both times."

"Exactly." He drummed his thumbs against the bar. "As a PI, I feel kind of amateur that I allowed someone to track my truck."

"First of all, we're not sure about that. Second, why would you think someone would slap a GPS on your truck? If he's involved with this case, the Keldorf case or both, he wouldn't have to be a genius to figure out, both times, where we were going. Watching us head to Whidbey, he must've figured we were coming here to talk to Nate." Hannah raised her finger in the air. "You care if I order another glass of wine? The first one barely made a dent in my nervous system."

"Go ahead." Jed plowed a hand through his hair. "What I don't understand is why kill Nate? Why not try to prevent us from talking to him in the first place? How did this guy know Nate wasn't going to spill the beans to us at our first meeting? If Nate had told us during our first conversation about this Adam, or whoever, he didn't need to die."

"Maybe Nate's killer was following us here on the island. If he were waiting for us outside the liquor store or saw our interaction with Nate inside, he would've known we didn't get what we came here for. He could've watched us get a bite to eat, watched Nate try to close up his store and figured we were going back." Hannah thanked the bartender for her second glass of wine and took a small sip. "Or maybe it was just revenge for talking to us."

"I didn't even ask if you knew an Adam on Dead Falls."

"If that's even what Nate was trying to say. Maybe Aidan." Hannah ran a finger around the rim of her glass. "It's a start, though. When we get back, I'm going to get Maggie's help and start digging into the files on the Keldorfs' foster children and their families."

"Do you think she'll allow it? Will it get her into trouble?"

Hannah patted her chest. "I'm a child therapist. I'm treating two children of murdered parents. I could easily get access if I went through the proper channels. Maggie knows this. She won't deny me."

Jed cocked his head at Hannah. That second glass of wine was going to her head. "Why wouldn't you go through proper channels?"

"It would take too long. It's sort of like how PIs can make

inroads where the police can't." She raised her glass to her lips and winked. "We don't have to play by the same rules."

Jed raised his eyebrows. "Okay, we need to get out of here and get back to Dead Falls. I'm sure Chu is going to have some questions for us about Nate's murder...or at least he should."

Hannah thunked down her glass suddenly. "Are we late? Do we still have a ride back to Dead Falls?"

"I texted my guy a while ago. He's good for any time. He has a place to stay on Dead Falls when he makes late runs like this." He tapped her glass. "Finish up if you still feel like you need it. Don't worry. I'll keep you steady on the boat—or least keep you from falling overboard."

"Thanks." She pressed a hand over her eyes. "Although I'm not sure I'm ever going to get the picture of Nate and all that blood out of my head."

He covered her hand with his. "I know. I'm sorry you had to see it. I'm even sorrier we led Nate's killer to his store."

"I feel guilty, too." Hannah gulped. "But how could we know we were putting his life in danger? Do you think that's another reason he changed his name? To escape this Ad person?"

"I don't know. He sure seemed nervous about someone, but if he knew who the real killer was, why didn't he tell the police years ago? Why allow that stain on his brother to stand?"

"I knew you were innocent. I just couldn't prove it." And with that, Hannah drained her glass.

The ride back to Dead Falls was cold and miserable, and Jed gave up his jacket to Hannah, keeping his arm locked around her trembling frame. When they docked, he gave a sigh of relief when he spotted his truck in the parking lot under a light. With someone following them, he didn't know what he expected.

He unlocked the doors with the key fob, and then handed it to Hannah. "Hop inside and start the engine to get the heater going."

"What are you doing?"

"I'm going to check for a tracker." He held up his cell phone. "I still have a detector on my phone from my PI days in LA."

"This I gotta see."

Jed crouched down and directed his phone along the chassis of his truck as he squat-walked around the back of it. His phone started beeping, and he reached into the wheel well and felt around the oily surface. His fingers stumbled across a plastic rectangle, and he yanked it from the undercarriage.

He rose to his feet, cupping the device in his palm where it caught the light from above. "Bingo."

THE FOLLOWING MORNING, Hannah groaned and dragged a pillow over her face. Two glasses of wine and a murder had left her dehydrated, drained and desperate. When she didn't feel Siggy's morning presence, she opened one eye and squinted at the foot of her bed. She cleared her throat and rasped, "Siggy, kitty."

Rolling to her side, she caught sight of a glass of water on her nightstand and a dark green gelcap. As she sat up to grab the water, the distinct aroma of bacon wafted up the stairs and floated into her bedroom.

No wonder Siggy had hightailed it downstairs. Hannah curled her hand around the glass and popped the ibuprofen in her mouth, swallowing it with a gulp of water.

Jed had insisted on staying the night with her and had

also insisted on sleeping in the spare room, despite her best efforts to seduce him into her bed. He had a firm rule about not sleeping with women who were over the legal limit.

She downed the rest of the water and scooted out of bed. As she tottered down the stairs, gripping the banister, she called out, "You didn't have to make breakfast."

When she reached the kitchen, Jed turned with a pair of tongs in his hand and Siggy twirling around his ankles. He snapped the tongs together. "Siggy made me do it."

"You'd better not be feeding that cat any bacon." She shook her finger at him, and then inhaled the scent of the coffee brewing. "But I can forgive you since you did make coffee and leave me some water."

He pointed to the kitchen table, set with the sunflower place mats and a jar of flowers in the center. "Sit."

Pulling out a chair, she raised her eyebrows. "How long have you been up, and when did you get so domestic?"

"I'm trying." He held up the pot of coffee. "Cream? Sugar?"

"The works, but grab me some sweetener." She planted an elbow on the table and balanced her chin in her palm. "How do you have so much energy after the night we had?"

"I wish you meant that in a good way." He winked at her. "I already talked to Chu this morning. He's not happy that we went looking for Nate Keldorf."

"Of course he isn't, but does he admit now that the Keldorf murder is somehow connected to these current murders?"

Jed lifted his shoulders as he delivered a mug of coffee to her, the surface a swirl of white cream. He dropped several packets of sweetener on the table next to the cup. "He said he's going to put a guy on it."

"One guy?" She ripped open a packet and dumped the crystals into her coffee.

"They're busy tracking down a woman who complained about Chase Thompson."

"You told him Nate's dying words about someone named Ad, right?"

"I did." Jed laid out the remaining bacon on some paper towel and divided the scrambled eggs between two plates. "Can you find out the names of the surviving Keldorf fosters today?"

"I think I can. Maggie doesn't play it by the book all the time. I'm sure she can get me in the database."

"I think it's about time we get the story from those two. Find out if they know someone named Adam or Aidan, or something like that." He sat beside her and dug his fork into the pile of yellow eggs on his plate. "They're probably not going to be too happy about being tracked down, but maybe they'll be more willing to talk to us than the cops, anyway."

"Yeah, 'cause we did such a great job with Nate." She slurped up some coffee, her eyes meeting Jed's over the rim.

"Not our fault, Hannah." He pushed her plate toward her. "Eat. We're going to have a busy day."

When they finished breakfast, Jed had a few appointments to get to—including a stop to buy ammo for her gun. After watching Nate bleed out last night in the back of his store, Hannah didn't think Jed was overreacting anymore.

After she cleaned up the kitchen and fed Siggy a proper meal, she showered and dressed in work clothes. Then she went out to her office, taking that thumb drive from her father's things with her. In between a little work, she planned to plug that in and see what her father felt was so important to keep from Jed's case.

As she inserted the key into the dead bolt, a snap of twigs had her spinning around, clutching the keys like a weapon.

Dr. Robbins held up his hands. "Sorry. Did I frighten you?"

His unctuous smile did nothing to slow down her pulse. She pressed a hand to her heart that was thumping in her chest. Why did she think his face was pleasant? "Dr. Robbins! You did scare me. Where did you come from?"

She peered over his shoulder, hoping to see someone else with him. How did he even know she had her office back here—out of sight of the road?

"I was just driving by on my way to my office, saw your car out front and thought I'd drop in."

Hannah tilted her head. There were probably about three things wrong with his explanation, but she wasn't going to cross-examine him. She licked her dry lips and stood in front of her office door. If she had to make a run for it, she didn't want to be trapped in that office with only one way in and out.

"The children? Did you want to discuss the children?"

He shifted from one foot to the other, the soles of his expensive shoes out of place on the unpaved entrance to her office. "Not the children so much, but the…mothers."

He just couldn't get over those unfit mothers. She buried her hand in the folds of her voluminous skirt, still clutching her keys between her fingers. "If you know something about the mothers, you should probably talk to the sheriff's department."

"Oh, not in that way." He rubbed at a spot on his forehead, brushing a dark curl out of the way. "I just want to clarify what I meant yesterday when I said those kids might be better off without their mothers. I didn't mean that the way it sounded."

"It sounded…"

"Cruel and unfeeling." He hung his head, as if in shame, but the quick glance up to monitor her response ruined it. "Sometimes when I talk to other professionals about patients, I lose my bedside manner. You know, I treat children who have injuries and illness due to neglectful parents. Sometimes I direct that anger at the parents—only in my head. I didn't want you to get the wrong impression."

If he didn't want her to get the wrong impression, he should've never shown up at her place like this. "I understand. We all see things we'd rather not. It's difficult not to blame the parents, but…"

"You're absolutely right. We can judge them, but nobody deserved to die like those two women did." He brushed a speck of something from his jacket. "Did we clear the air?"

"I'm not sure it needed clearing, Dr. Robbins." She turned her body sideways to her office door. "I do need to get to work."

"Of course. I've heard such good reports of you. Sorry to take up so much of your time." He crunched back down the path, and then cranked his head over his shoulder. "You'll let me know if you need to consult with me about those children."

"Yes, I will." She held her breath until he disappeared about the corner. Then she pushed into her office, slammed the door behind her and locked it. "That was creepy."

She sank into the chair she used with the older kids. She usually sat on the floor with the young ones. A white disk slipped onto the floor and bounced onto the area rug. She dropped to her knees to retrieve it.

After discovering the tracker on Jed's truck, she'd had the bright idea of putting one of those GPS tags in Sheldon's shoe and tracking it on her phone, in case he took flight again. She slipped the disk into her pocket and backed up into the chair again as she placed a call to Maggie. She listened to the recorded message before leaving her own.

She patted the other pocket of her skirt and pulled out her father's thumb drive. As she made a move toward her laptop, Maggie called her back.

"Hey, Maggie. Did that message make sense to you?"

"It did. Don't you already have a log-in to the CPS database?"

"Only on an as-needed basis depending on my patient."

"Well, I'd say this is one of those cases. Both of those children have files with CPS. No reason why you shouldn't get in there and look at them."

"Thanks, Maggie. How do we do that?" Hannah bit her bottom lip. She didn't say, and Maggie didn't correct her, that she had access only through a social worker, usually Maggie, who printed out the files for her.

Maggie huffed out a breath. "Look, I can talk to IT about a temp password, but that could take forever. You can use my log-in credentials."

Hannah collapsed back into the deep, soft chair. "Thanks. You're a lifesaver."

"No, you're a lifesaver for those kids, Hannah Maddox. I'll e-mail you the link and my username and password. How many days do you think you'll need? I'm going to have to change my password when you're done. You understand."

"Absolutely. Give me two days, Maggie."

"You got it. Relatives of Sheldon and Chrissy are incoming any day now. It will be up to them to decide if they want the kids to continue their sessions with you."

"If they don't, I can recommend someone wherever they land with those children."

"Excellent. Look out for the e-mail, and I'll talk to you soon."

Hannah tilted her head back and yelled at the ceiling. "Yes!"

She launched out of the chair and swept the laptop from her desk. She brought it back to the chair with her, balanced it on the overstuffed arm and powered it on.

She drummed her fingers on the keyboard, waiting for Maggie's e-mail to come through. As she watched the blinking cursor, she burrowed into her skirt pocket and pulled out the thumb drive. She skimmed her fingers along the side of her computer, feeling for the port. Tracing the rectangular opening, she fed the thumb drive into the side of the laptop.

She double-clicked to open the file and blinked at some security footage that showed the front of a store.

Her computer dinged at her, and she switched to her e-mail. She double clicked on Maggie's message, copied and pasted the link she'd been sent into a browser and entered Maggie's username and password. She rubbed her hands together as she watched the CPS database come to life on her screen.

Hannah ran the cursor across the tabs at the top of the window and zeroed in on the archives tab. She hadn't confirmed with Maggie, but she hoped the archives went back thirty years. She clicked on the green tab, and a list of year ranges popped up on the screen.

With her breath coming in short spurts, she scrolled down and clicked on the link for the Keldorf murder years. The tab for the Keldorf family jumped out at her immediately. They'd had a long, successful history with CPS as foster parents, but it had ended in disaster. They exhibited no problems before this massacre. CPS wasn't a law enforcement agency, so the database included just a brief summary of the facts—but she knew the facts. She wanted names.

Hunching forward, she trailed her finger down the screen, jabbing it when she reached the family. She read them aloud. "Chet Keldorf, his wife—Sheila Keldorf—and the kids at the time of the murders. Four-year-old Selina, six-year-old Jacob—both dead—and the surviving siblings… Alyssa Abbott, thirteen, and her biological brother Addison Abbott, fifteen."

Hannah grabbed a notepad and pen from the end table beside the chair and scribbled down the siblings' names. Her pen jerked across the page. Addison Abbott? Not Adam. Addison.

Nate Keldorf didn't fear the parents of one of these foster kids—he feared the kid.

Chapter Eighteen

"Hannah, are you in there?" Jed tapped on the door of Hannah's office. She hadn't mentioned a morning patient, but she could be in there with someone.

The door flew open so fast, Jed stumbled back a step. "Whoa! A-are you alone?"

"I'm alone, and I just discovered something." She grabbed his arm and practically dragged him across the threshold into the cozy space that looked like a child's dream playroom.

She grabbed her laptop and spun around, thrusting the computer in front of her. "I'm in the CPS archive database. Do you see this?"

He squinted at the screen as she jerked it back and forth in the air. "No, I can't see anything. You're waving it around."

"Sit." She patted the cushion of a big comfy chair, and he sank into it. Then she placed the laptop on his knees and jabbed a finger at the screen. "Look at the names of the Keldorf fosters."

His gaze tracked down the page, and he sucked in a breath when he saw the name of the fifteen-year-old boy. "Addison. Do you think that's the name Nate was trying to spit out?"

"It has to be, don't you think? That's too much of a coincidence. It's the boy, Jed. That's why my father had circled the surviving foster kids. He suspected something."

"Maybe Addison, the boy, is a junior. Maybe the little ones have a father with the bio name of Adam. There could be a lot of possibilities here, Hannah."

"I know." She waved her hands in the air as if shooing away those possibilities. "Addison Abbott would be about forty-five years old now. Any bio parent would be closer to sixty-five. What's more likely? A forty-five-year-old taking vengeance or a sixty-five-year-old?"

"But taking vengeance against whom?" He tapped her screen. "If Nate Keldorf suspected Addison Abbott of killing the family, it sounds like the kid already got his vengeance for whatever Chet Keldorf did to him and his sister."

"It's symbolic, Jed. These killings are symbolic. Addison sees children being mistreated like he was, and he's rescuing them from their home life." Hannah pressed a hand against her chest, her eyes blinking.

"What's wrong?"

"Dr. Robbins is about midforties."

"Are we back to Robbins?"

"He came to my office earlier. Said he wanted to clear the air about the statement he made regarding Zoey and Stephanie—about their being unfit mothers and their kids better off without them."

"He came *here*?" Jed patted the bag in his jacket pocket that contained the bullets for the Glock he'd cleaned for Hannah. "Did he change his name from Addison Abbott to Robbins?"

"Bob or Robert Robbins." She squeezed beside him on the chair and dragged the computer to her lap. She clicked through the database, scrolled through files and entered words in the search field. "I'm pretty sure Addison Abbott changed his name...but I don't think his sister Alyssa did. She shows up a few more times in this database as Alyssa Abbott, but Addison never makes another appearance."

"Alyssa might know where her brother is, but she's never going to talk to the police. Is there any information where she might be located now?"

"It doesn't say. She'd been in a few group homes." Hannah shook her head and sniffed. "That Chet Keldorf must've done a number on those kids."

"Whatever Keldorf did was only amplified by what her brother did—if he is responsible." He dragged the bag with the ammo out of his pocket and swung it from his fingertips. "I'm going to start tracking down Alyssa Abbott and see if I can get a line on Addison Abbott's new identity. You load your gun and keep it with you, in case Dr. Robbins, or anyone else, swings by again."

She wrapped her hand around the plastic, which crackled in her grip. "Do you think you can find the Abbotts?"

"I told you. I have some very shady but good sources." He quirked his eyebrows up and down.

"Ex-cons, you mean."

He held up his fingers in boy scout fashion and said, "I'm not an ex-con, so I'm not on parole and don't have those same restrictions. I can fraternize with whomever I please."

"Are these guys...?"

"Misunderstood." He kissed the side of her head. "What do you have on tap for the rest of the day?"

She took a quick glance down at her computer and the flash drive sticking out of the side before cupping her hand over it. "Some work to take care of, and I think the teachers at the elementary school might drop by to discuss how to move forward with the kids when they get back to school—if they get back to school."

He recognized the flash drive from Sheriff Maddox's collection of junk. He had no idea what Hannah was trying to prove or disprove about his case.

"Why wouldn't the kids be back in school? Too soon?" He kissed her again, his lips lingering on her soft hair, before hauling himself out of the deep chair.

"Maggie told me relatives are swooping in for Sheldon and Chrissy. They may take them out of the area."

"Might not be a bad idea." He poked at the bag in her lap. "Load that gun. I'm not kidding."

"I will. Trust me."

She trailed him to the door of her office, and once he was outside, he turned and kissed her on the mouth. "I do trust you, Hannah. That's why you don't have to pretend you're not still snooping into my case."

SEVERAL PHONE CALLS, web searches, records searches, lies and payoffs later, Jed was headed for Alyssa Abbott's group home just outside Seattle. He'd driven onto the ferry from Dead Falls to Whidbey and then took another ferry to Seattle. The forty-minute drive from Seattle to Carnation should get him there before sunset.

He did not, however, have the same luck with Addison Abbott. Alyssa's brother must've definitely changed his name because he dropped off the face of the earth immediately after the massacre of the Keldorf family.

The drive took him from the city to tree-lined roads and rural landscapes. The group home where Alyssa resided housed nonviolent, mentally disturbed adults. He hoped that Alyssa was cognizant enough to give him information about Addison.

A stately home with cottages scattered around its perimeter met him around the next bend. He drank in the beauty and peacefulness of the scene. Anyone who'd come out of that Keldorf nightmare, detailed in the CPS database, deserved this—he just hoped he didn't have to ruin it for Alyssa.

He pulled up in front of the big house and nodded to a maintenance worker as he got out of the car. He figured he'd have to check in with the staff before approaching Alyssa. Maybe Hannah should've been the one to visit Alyssa Abbott. At least she had some credentials as a psychologist and a reason for being here.

He took a deep breath of the pine-scented air and jogged up the steps to the front door. The front room looked like a hotel lobby but instead of a long counter for check-in, an antique desk was tucked in the corner with a woman on a computer behind it.

He ran his hands down the lapels of his jacket. He'd figured a jacket and a pair of slacks would present a better image than his regular jeans and T-shirt.

The woman looked up from her computer, and he gave her his best smile while reading her nameplate. "Good afternoon, Ms. Bullard."

"Hello." She shoved her glasses to the tip of her nose and peered at him over the top of the frames.

"I'm here to visit someone today, Alyssa Abbott, and was hoping you could direct me to her cottage." He pulled out his wallet, ready to show her some ID.

The woman screwed up one side of her mouth and tapped the keyboard in front of her. "Name, please?"

"Jed Swain. I'm an old friend of Alyssa's, and her brother told me she was staying here."

Ms. Bullard was shaking her head before he even finished speaking. "You're not on her visitor list, Mr. Swain. I'm afraid you have to be on the visitor list to get access to Alyssa."

"Oh, I thought her brother had cleared me. I told him I was going to be passing through Seattle and wanted to take a detour to Carnation—just to check up on Alyssa. He said he'd set it up for me."

"He didn't." She drummed her fingers on the desk. "If you can get Mr. Abbott on the phone, I'll allow him to give me verbal approval."

Jed pulled out his phone as if he could actually make a call to Alyssa's brother. And if he'd been hoping to get Addison's real name here, it looked like he was facing disappointment in that area, too. The staff here knew him as Abbott.

Not wanting to push or raise any alarms, Jed backed off and waved his phone at Ms. Bullard. "I'll give him a call right now to see what I can do. I'd sure hate to miss this opportunity to see Alyssa."

Grasping his phone, he exited the building and turned the corner of the building. He gazed out at the individual cottages. If he were lucky, she'd be located in one of those instead of occupying a room in the main building.

With his phone to his ear, in case Ms. Bullard saw him out the window, he wandered toward the cottages. He glanced at the red door of the first structure. It had a number but no name on the front. Of course, it couldn't be that easy.

He meandered to a few more, peering into one window at a youngish man watching TV and another where an older couple chatted with a young woman with a child. He loped down a gentle dip toward a creek where two cottages crouched by the shore. He was about to approach one of the houses to see if he could peek through the crack in the curtains when the rustling and chirping of birds stopped him.

He veered toward the cottage from which the noises were emanating and stumbled to a stop when he saw a birdcage in front of an open window. He crept closer, and his heart tripped in his chest when he recognized two caged finches. What were the odds?

The door of number nine beckoned, and he stationed himself in front of it and tapped lightly. A silver-haired woman appeared in front of him, the lift of her lips the only expression on her face. If her hair had been black or brown, she could've passed for someone much younger at first glance, but at second and third glance Jed could tell her hair had turned gray prematurely.

He cleared his throat. "Hello, I heard your birds singing. Finches, aren't they?"

She nodded. "I like finches."

"So do I." He held out his hand. "I'm Jed."

Glancing down at his hand, she put her own behind her back. "Hello."

"What's your name?"

She stared past his shoulder for so long, he turned to see what she saw—nobody and nothing.

He tried again. "What's your name?"

Her brown eyes flickered. "Alyssa."

Jed eased out a slow breath. "Can I see your birds, Alyssa?"

She looked beyond him, into the distance again and widened the door. "You can see my finches."

"Thank you." He made sure to give her a wide berth.

She seemed as if she could take flight suddenly, like one of her birds.

Crooking her finger at him, she tiptoed toward the birdcage where the finches fluttered and tweeted. "They don't like loud noises. Neither do I."

He followed her to the cages and poked a finger between the wires. "They're nice birds. I like finches. I had finches once. My brother gave them to me. I kept them in a cage like this one. Where did you get your birds, Alyssa? Did you get them from your brother?"

She shook her head back and forth, her silver locks dancing on her shoulders. "My brother hates birds."

"So does mine. That's why he gave them to me." Jed stepped away from the cage and surveyed the neat room, furnished in pastel colors with framed Impressionist prints on the walls and shelves filled with books and miniatures. "What's your brother's name, Alyssa? My brother's name is… Bob."

Alyssa folded her hands in front of her. "My birds' names are Birdy and Tweep. What are you birds' names?"

"Ah, Siggy and Hannah." He sent Hannah a silent apology. "What about your brother? What's his name?"

"I was making dinner. Do you want dinner?"

"Yes, please." Anything to get her out of the room. Although in her state, it might not even register that he was looking around.

"Do you like soup?"

"I love soup. Thank you."

The knots in his gut loosened a little when she traipsed toward a small kitchen. He zeroed in on the shelves, studying the miniatures, which turned out to be photos of random Victorians. He plucked out a few books and shook their pages. His gaze darted to the wall. A collection of school class photos was bunched together beneath a Monet, and he faced them. Could these be from Alyssa's school years? Would her brother be in these photos?

He squinted at the dates at the bottom of the photos and cocked his head. These were recent photos from the past few years. Did Alyssa have a child in school? His pulse thrummed when he saw Samish Elementary next to the date. Did Alyssa have a child in school on Dead Falls Island? Did she have a niece or nephew?

He scanned the children's names beneath the photos, but none jumped out, except for Sheldon's, Chrissy's and Olly's. Two adult pictures graced each of the classroom photos—the classroom teacher and the principal, Mr. Lamar.

Jed planted a finger below Lamar's photo. He'd seen this guy before at Luigi's Pizza, talking to Hannah. He'd wanted to discuss how to handle Sheldon's and Chrissy's return to school. In fact, Hannah expected the teachers today.

His pulse thumped in his ears. Why would Alyssa have these classroom pictures? Who was the one constant in these pictures?

"Here's your soup."

Jed spun around, startling Alyssa so that the soup sloshed over the sides of the bowls into the plates.

Holding out his hands, he said, "I'm sorry, Alyssa."

She put the soup down on the coffee table and wiped her hands on the frilly apron tied around her waist. "You're looking at my pictures."

"They're nice." He jerked his thumb over his shoulder at the wall. "Is that your brother in those pictures, Alyssa?"

"Oh, yes." She tugged on her apron. "My brother is the principal of Samish Elementary School."

Chapter Nineteen

Hannah sighed as she slid her key into the lock on her office door and pushed it open. Minutes after Jed left to find Alyssa Abbott, Hannah had gotten called out on an emergency for one of her teenaged patients. The poor boy had attempted suicide, and Hannah had spent the rest of the afternoon with him and his family at the hospital.

Caleb's issues had kept her engaged and busy all day, but the thumb drive in her laptop had occupied one corner of her mind throughout the ordeal with Caleb. While at the hospital, she'd realized that the security footage on the file belonged to Jerry's 24/7, the convenience store where Jed had gone the night Zoey accused him of rape.

The Dead Falls Sheriff's Department couldn't verify Jed's alibi for that night because Jerry's security camera had malfunctioned and law enforcement couldn't view his tapes. What was her father doing with security footage from Jerry's 24/7 if it wasn't any good?

She dropped her bag on the floor at the corner of her desk and folded herself into the chair, dragging the computer into her lap. She tapped the keyboard to wake up the laptop and clicked on the security footage file.

The grainy images appeared with the lights of an occasional passing car illuminating the front parking lot. One set of lights grew bigger and brighter, and the footage showed the nose of a pickup truck parking in front of the store. Hannah sucked in a breath.

Seconds later, a figure emerged from the truck. The young man scooped a hand through his dark hair, pushing it back from his handsome face. She'd know that face anywhere.

Jed took a few steps toward the entrance of the convenience store, patting his back pocket. He stopped, felt in his other pockets for the missing wallet and pivoted back to his truck.

Hannah whispered under her breath, "Keep going, Jed. Go into the store so Jerry can see you."

The lights from Jed's truck blazed on again and dimmed as he pulled out of the parking lot.

Hannah's gaze darted to the timestamp on the video. She fell against the back of the chair, her hand over her mouth. The time gave Jed his alibi. Her father had stolen the tape from Jerry's 24/7 and replaced it with a bum tape to frame Jed for Zoey's rape.

A sharp rap on the door of her office made her jerk upright. Could it be Jed already? He'd texted her that he'd found the location of Alyssa's group home and was heading out there. She hadn't heard from him since.

She clambered out of the chair and flew to the door. She threw it open, and the disappointment of seeing Bryan Lamar on her porch punched her in the gut. She'd forgotten about the meeting today.

"Oh, hey, Bryan. Come on in." She peered over his broad shoulder into the darkness. "Are the kids' teachers coming?"

"Yeah, they're right behind me." He stepped across the

threshold of her office and gave her space a quick glance. "No patients, I hope."

Tilting her head, she said, "I wouldn't have invited you in if there were."

How was she going to sit through this meeting with the knowledge she had about Jed's alibi weighing down her heart? She had to tell him before she did anything else.

Holding up her index finger, she said, "Just give me one minute before we start. I need to make a quick call. I'll be done before the others get here."

She turned to grab her bag from the floor, but Bryan brushed past her and kicked the bag out of her reach.

She gave a nervous laugh. "Are you okay? Did you trip?"

Bryan scooped up the bag and snatched her phone from the side pocket.

She extended her hand, wiggling her fingers. "Thanks, Bryan."

He pressed his thumb against the side of her phone and tossed it onto the chair.

She blinked. What the hell was he doing? Did he think she was one of his students or something?

"I really need to make a phone call, Bryan. Just before the others come." She made a move toward the chair, and he moved his bulky frame in front of her.

"The others aren't coming, Hannah, and you're not getting your phone."

Her mouth dropped open as the hair on the back of her neck quivered. "Wh-what are you talking about, Bryan? What are you doing?"

She shuffled back toward her desk and the heavy paperweight on the edge.

Bryan pulled a gun out of his pocket and aimed it at her

head. "Just stop, Hannah. That little rock on your desk is no match for my weapon."

"I don't understand what's going on." But the terror throbbing at the base of her spine told her it wasn't good.

"Really? At the moment of truth, you play dumb? Did your jailbird boyfriend find my sister? Did he think her home wouldn't call me to ask me about my *friend* paying her a visit?"

Knots twisted in her gut, and she put a fist against her midsection. "You're Addison Abbott."

"And you're not going to tell anyone." He waved the gun at her. "Get moving."

Her hands clenched into fists as she eyed her phone on the cushion of the chair.

"Don't even think about it. I turned it off, anyway. You're not going to make a grab for it and call 911—not before I shoot you." His hand steadied, and he nodded toward her purse on the floor next to her bag. "Get your purse and walk out the door ahead of me. Lock the door behind you."

"You're going to make this look like I left on my own?" She pointed to her dead phone. "Not without my cell phone."

Shrugging, he said, "People leave their phones behind all the time. Go."

She turned and crouched to pick up her purse. She could turn and swing it at him, but if a rock was no match for a gun, then a purse was even less of one. Bryan didn't want to shoot her here and leave evidence behind, and that was going to buy her some time.

Hitching the purse over her shoulder, she shuffled toward the door. If only she had talked to Jed when she got back instead of pouncing on that thumb drive. If he had talked to

Alyssa and discovered Bryan's identity, he could've warned her, and she never would've let Bryan in her office.

She opened the door and peered outside, hopeful that Jed was on his way back to Dead Falls right now. Maybe they'd pass him on the road, even though she had no idea where Bryan was taking her.

Her low-heeled boots crunched on the gravel as she walked toward the car parked on the side of her house. Nobody could see the car from her driveway, and her security cameras didn't include this area. She'd wanted to afford her patients some privacy and had never had cameras pointing at her office. Jed would have no idea what happened to her or where she went.

A sob caught in her throat, but she stifled it. She had to stay on an even keel while dealing with Bryan. Maybe she could talk him out of killing her. Give him a chance to get away.

As she got in the passenger side of his car, Bryan crowded behind her and pushed her forward. "You drive, and if you try to veer off the road or into another car, I'll shoot you."

She believed him. She crawled over the console with Bryan's gun jabbed into her back and settled behind the wheel. "Where to?"

"I'll give you directions as we go."

Her attempts to engage him in conversation and ask questions hung between them in the car, as the only words he spoke were curt directions. After several minutes of seeing no other cars on the road, Hannah didn't need Bryan's directions anymore. He was taking her to the falls.

As they crossed the bridge, she debated briefly aiming the car into the guardrail, but there was something very attractive about staying alive right now, for as many minutes as possible.

Once across the bridge, he directed her to an overhang where his car would be out of sight of anyone crossing the bridge. She parked.

"Now what?"

"Out of the car." He backed out of the passenger side, keeping the gun trained on her, and motioned for her to crawl across the console again. He pointed to the path that led to the back side of the falls. "You know the way."

She was sure she knew this path a lot better than he did. As they got close to the water, the cold spray tickled her face and clung to her hair.

They faced each other on the narrow path behind the falls, the water roaring in Hannah's ears. They each had one of the caves behind them. Hers was farther away, but she might be able to take a few steps back and throw herself to the side. Of course, that could all go horribly wrong if she slipped on the slick path beneath her feet or Bryan shot her before she could gain the safety of the cave.

She licked her lips, the moisture giving her dry mouth a much-needed salve. "Why, Bryan? Why did you kill Zoey and Stephanie? What did they ever do to you?"

Bryan rolled his shoulders, his grip on the gun relaxing. Now that he had her where he wanted her, he had more confidence, and that confidence would loosen his lips.

"They didn't do anything to me, but they were harming their children, day in and day out. I could see it at school, and I saw the CPS reports."

She asked, "Why did you pick on single mothers? What about the terrible fathers?"

"Their dirtbag fathers were already out of the picture,

had already abandoned their kids. Believe me, if I found a single father neglecting his child, I would've taken him out, too. You're a child psychologist. Tell me that neglect, that abuse, doesn't bother you."

Bryan was lying. He's too cowardly to confront a man. Vulnerable women were so much easier to kill, but she didn't want to anger him. "Of course, it bothers me, but there are methods."

He snorted. "Methods. The only surefire method is to take out the abuser."

"Like you took out Chet Keldorf, your foster father?" She held her breath and inched back a little toward the cave behind her.

"Damn right." His hand gripped the gun harder, and a muscle twitched in his jaw. "He didn't want children. He wanted victims. He locked us in that pen in the barn. You know. You saw it, didn't you? H-he sexually abused my sister and the other girls. That's why my sister is in that home. He ruined her life. He had to pay."

"And Mrs. Keldorf? Sheila?"

"She helped him. She was as evil as he was—and those damned birds. He cared about those birds more than his foster children."

"But what about the little ones? Why Selina and Jacob?"

"They were innocents, but they didn't have a chance at a life after being with the Keldorfs. I showed them a mercy."

Hannah's stomach turned, and she shoved her hands in her pockets. Her fingers touched a small disk—the GPS tag meant for Sheldon. Her heart leapt in her chest. Her phone was tracking her location. She had to keep him talking.

"I—I can understand that, Bryan. I've seen it myself.

Some children are just too far gone to be saved, but you saved your sister."

He narrowed his eyes at her unexpected response. "I did save her."

"And you can save her now. If you kill me, you're not going to get away with it. What's going to happen to Alyssa when you're in prison?"

"You're wrong. I will get away with it and the others." He glanced at the rushing water, and Hannah knew she had only a few minutes.

"Nate Keldorf."

Bryan shrugged. "He suspected me. He knew what went on in that house and did nothing."

"You killed him on a busy street. Do you really believe the police aren't going to find some clues to connect you to that murder?"

He gestured toward the water crashing next to them. "You're going to jump. Suicide. Happens all the time out here. Maybe you discovered your ex-con boyfriend was really guilty of rape, and you couldn't handle the truth."

"We took your car. When you drive away, law enforcement is going to wonder how I got here." Could she reason with a madman?

The slightest movement behind Bryan caught her eye. The relief she felt at seeing Jed poke his head from the cave behind Bryan almost made her knees weak, and she had to place a hand against the damp rock beside her to steady herself.

Jed had snuck into the caves from a path where the falls gathered for their descent. Not many people knew about that path and fewer attempted to traverse it.

"Y-you could've walked here, or maybe they'll never find your body."

She'd rattled him and his little plan. He hadn't thought of everything. He had to be wondering what else he missed.

"Bryan, we can work this out together. I was no fan of Zoey's. She lied about Jed, almost ruined his life. I could see that Stephanie Boyd was a terrible mother. I can help those kids now. I won't tell anyone, but you have to promise you'll stop. If you stop, I can let the others go."

He took a step toward her. "You can jump, or I'll shoot you first and you'll topple over. Your choice, Hannah."

Jed emerged from the cave but if Bryan sensed him there, they'd all die.

"Wait!" She thrust out a hand to stop Bryan's forward movement. "What about Astrid? Why'd you kidnap Olly?"

"I wasn't ready for my next kill yet—Vera Allende. She left the island in the middle of my planning stages. Astrid was just to keep the cops on their toes. She needed a warning, anyway. She had a record with CPS. It could've been true. She's keeping her son from his father."

"You had access to all the CPS records, didn't you? As principal, you have your kill list at your fingertips."

"I'm tired of talking, Hannah. We both know you're not going to help me or keep quiet. And that boyfriend of yours will never keep quiet, either."

Jed took that as a signal and launched toward Bryan on the narrow, slippery path. "Hannah, move!"

As the two men fell to the ground, Hannah jumped back and threw herself to the side to reach the cave. Her hip hit the edge, and her feet scrambled for purchase on the path.

She screamed as Bryan, with Jed on top of him, rolled toward the cliff's rim. Bryan still had the gun clutched in his hand, but Jed had his knee on Bryan's elbow so that he couldn't move his arm.

Bryan bucked beneath Jed, lifting him in the air. Jed grabbed on to a branch jutting from the hillside as Bryan clambered to his knees and freed his arm. He swung the gun toward Jed.

Hannah screamed again, dropping to a crouch, ready to crawl toward Bryan.

As Bryan took aim, Jed kicked out with one leg, his foot landing in the middle of Bryan's chest. Bryan's eyes rounded, both of his arms windmilling at his sides as he attempted to keep his balance.

He failed, and the waters of Dead Falls swept him into their embrace.

Epilogue

The fire crackled, and Hannah extended her legs to the warmth, wiggling her toes in her boots. "Autumn snuck in here and knocked summer right off her throne."

Jed dragged his chair next to hers, cupping his mug of coffee. "Almost time for me to start the academy."

"We're excited to have you, Jed. Although why they hold an academy right during one of the worst times for fire out here is beyond me." Tate clapped Jed on the back. "You sure you wanna give up your PI work? You're a natural."

"I'll keep my license handy." He squeezed Hannah's knee. "I have to try to keep this one out of trouble."

"I wouldn't have been in trouble if you hadn't dragged me into your investigation."

"Is that what I did? Seems to me you're the natural."

Hannah brought his hand to her lips and kissed his knuckles. She'd told him about finding the tape recording his alibi among her father's things. He'd always known her father had set him up, and now he knew how he'd done it.

Astrid tugged on her son's sleeve. "Go get your uncle some water."

"I don't need…" Tate stopped when he saw his sister's face. "Grab me a bottle from the fridge, Olly."

When Olly disappeared into the house, Astrid hugged her jacket to her body and gave an exaggerated shiver. "To think that Mr. Lamar went to the trouble of getting Olly's phone number to involve him in his sick games makes me ill."

"If it makes you feel any better, I don't think Lamar had you in his sights as a victim. He'd already picked out Vera Allende." Hannah shook her hair back from her face. "Not that that's a good thing. It astounds me that a fifteen-year-old boy was able to kill his whole family and pass it off as a murder-suicide."

Tate spread his hands. "Because who's going to suspect a scared teenaged foster kid of those brutal murders. And the kids."

Astrid covered her face with her hands. "So horrible. How are Sheldon and Chrissy?"

"Sheldon's grandparents are going to take him to Bend, and Chrissy is going to stay with her grandmother. Poor babies. They never did see Lamar, and they're lucky they didn't."

Olly returned outside with Tate's bottle of water and tossed it to him.

As Tate caught the bottle, he said, "I'm heading inside. I have some work to do. Good night, Hannah."

Astrid jumped from her chair. "You're not going to stick around for my world-famous s'mores?"

Tate patted his flat stomach. "I don't need any s'mores, world-famous or not."

"Come and help me." She grabbed Olly's hand and they trailed after Tate into the cabin.

The fire popped, and Hannah shivered.

"Are you cold?" Jed tugged on her arm, pulled her into

his lap and wrapped his arms around her. "After what happened at the falls, I don't feel like I ever want to let you go."

"Please don't." She snuggled against his chest. "I am so happy you looked at my phone when you got to my office—and remembered the pass code."

"How could I forget the pass code?" He wedged a finger beneath her chin and kissed her. "I'm just glad that tracker app popped up on your phone when I got into it. I'm not sure I would've known where to look for that or would have even known you had that tag on you."

"It was just by chance that I slipped it into the pocket of my skirt that afternoon. When I discovered it on that path with Lamar, I hoped and prayed that you'd come to my office, find my phone and find me."

"Prayers answered." He nuzzled her neck. "I've had a lot of prayers answered lately. I'm on a lucky streak."

"I just—" she sniffed and wiped a tear from the corner of her eye "—I just can't believe what my father did to you. I'm so sorry."

"He must've set things up with Zoey in advance. I don't believe she was even raped. Do you think—" he sucked in his bottom lip "—do you think Zoey and your father were involved? Did he give her his watch as a gift, or was it payment for setting me up?"

She wrinkled her nose. "I don't even want to think about that. Did the police ever find out where Zoey's money came from? Did she really steal that drug money from Chase?"

"If they did find out, they didn't tell me. If she did steal it from Chase Thompson, she was playing a dangerous game."

"It seems as if she enjoyed dangerous games." Another tear rolled down her cheek. "I should've seen something, done something."

He caught the tear with the pad of his thumb. "We've been over this before. You couldn't have known and there's nothing you could've done about it, anyway. It's in the past, Hannah. Let's put it in the past. Can you do that and move into the future…with me?"

She threw her arms around his neck and rested her cheek against his hair, as black as a raven's wing. "That's the only future I can see—one with you in it."

And when he kissed her this time, there were no bars between them, real or imagined.

* * * * *

COMING SOON!

We really hope you enjoyed reading this book.
If you're looking for more romance
be sure to head to the shops when
new books are available on

Thursday 7th December

To see which titles are coming soon, please visit
millsandboon.co.uk/nextmonth

MILLS & BOON

LET'S TALK

Romance

For exclusive extracts, competitions and special offers, find us online:

 MillsandBoon

 @MillsandBoon

 @MillsandBoonUK

 @MillsandBoonUK

Get in touch on 01413 063 232